Year Of The Rabbit

I0564056

by:

Jerry Koufeldt

ISBN: 069211825X
ISBN-13: 978-0692118252

All inquiries:
JerryKoufeldt@gmail.com

I say unto you: one must still have chaos in oneself to be able to give birth to a dancing star. I say unto you: you still have chaos in yourselves. -Nietzsche "Thus Spoke Zarathustra"

Year of the Rabbit Foreword

Every writer, especially one on the slightly neurotic side (ahem, me), needs a trusted friend to rely on during the agonizing times of revision and editing stories. For me, that friend is Jerry. We have known each other for sixteen years now, having originally bonded over a mutual love of Tori Amos' music. That shared interest eventually developed into a writer relationship, each of us keeping the deep dark secrets of our worst work while celebrating accomplishments along the way.

Jerry is a very different writer than I am, and in this has some traits that I truly admire. For one, he writes what he thinks without hesitation, where I might let a story sit in the crock pot of words for months, sometimes even years, before writing it down. Where I am overly ornate and flowy, he knows where to pinch words and be concise. If I spend way too much time describing a teacup, Jerry isn't afraid to tell me. Because of watching his process, I have been able to improve my own work, and we have created that necessary trusted relationship of being writers and critics. Together, we have evolved in technique and style.

In *Year of the Rabbit*, the reader will come to know Jerry's style: part Americana, part futuristic. Writing is all about learning a craft and tailoring it throughout time. Writing comes with a lot of rules; however, every writer knows those rules can be broken. It isn't always easy to break those rules successfully, but *Year of the Rabbit* does. We live in a society where everything is immediate. We get news instantly. We can make an online order and have it delivered hours later. If we don't have the answer to a piece of obscure trivia, we can obtain it within seconds. When I was in graduate school, I was taught the same thing: place the reader in the middle of the story right away. Place the reader into the action, or else they will be bored.

I've had the pleasure of reading the stories within *Year of the Rabbit* many times, and one thing I appreciate about many of them is the delayed gratification. This is a rarity in modern society. For example, "Flea Market Lucy: The Bearded Lady's Daughter" opens with Lucy's unfortunate propensity for getting arrested. Lucy doesn't remember the circumstances of every arrest. As readers today, we might assume that Lucy is a bad person and deserved to get arrested, but we don't immediately know her position. We have to wait for it and travel with Lucy through her childhood to learn about those arrests. In the story following Lucy's, "The Frog Gig," the opening line is "We had a good night, but, well, we'll get to that." This is another area where we as readers need to wait for the action, and I promise that it is worth waiting for throughout this collection.

In *Year of the Rabbit*, prepare to be surprised, horrified, sad, and sentimental, and expect the lines between fiction and reality to be blurred. Expect to develop a curiosity about technology and how the future connects to the nostalgia of days before. Expect to travel to the heart of America and meet people living there, inhabiting small towns that crawl with character. When the reader thinks they can predict what is next, they will feel the brush of heat from a fiery kiln. Delight in the erratic and fortuitous journey with a touch of serendipity. -Melissa Chichester

CONTENTS

ACKNOWLEDGMENTS

Edited by: Melissa Chichester

Cover Layout and Design: Jonathan Ruth and Jerry Koufeldt

Cover Photography: Jerry Koufeldt

The Rabbit Of Waverly Hills

This story began in 1956. My uncle, while working at American Tobacco, was diagnosed with tuberculosis and admitted to Waverly Hills Sanatorium. He spent fifteen months there before he was released. This was nearing the end of the hospital's life. He was about twenty-two years old at the time, already married and had two children. The story goes his wife got pregnant while he was in the hospital. That sounds like a scandal, but it's not. That's part of the story. You see, Uncle Junie, that's his family nickname, was given a different nickname while he was in Waverly Hills. They called him "The Rabbit."

Waverly Hills

In 1910, Waverly Hills Sanatorium opened in Jefferson County, Kentucky to help the city of Louisville control an outbreak of the "white plague", tuberculosis. Local myths and legends estimate that over 100,000 people died in Waverly Hills in the 52 years it was open as a hospital. In truth, just over 8,000 people died there. I can't imagine how many people die annually in an average hospital in Kentucky with nearly 68% of the state's population being classified as obese today.

The outbreak of the white plague hit Louisville hard. Louisville has a lot of swamp-like conditions. It's not a dry area at all, especially in autumn and spring. The bacterium that causes tuberculosis thrives in the humid conditions of the Ohio Valley. The Ohio Valley is one of those places where in the summer, it might be 100 degrees and 90% humidity. Sitting in the shade doesn't do a lot against that kind of humidity. Everything is always wet; nothing dries out.

The original Waverly Hills building was a two-story wooden structure that held forty to fifty patients. Constant repairs to the wood structure and the need for expansion led to a more permanent five-story building that could hold four hundred patients in 1926. With the number of cases of tuberculosis declining after 1943 as a result of the antibiotic streptomycin, Waverly Hills Sanatorium closed in 1961.

The hospital did reopen in 1962 as Woodhaven Geriatrics Center. Woodhaven was a nursing home primarily used to care for elderly patients with dementia and the mentally disabled. Woodhaven was closed by the state of Kentucky in the early 80s, in rumor, due to the mistreatment and neglect of patients, which was often the case in such situations. This led to the over-romanticized urban legends surrounding the hauntings of what came to be inappropriately labeled an insane asylum.

Waverly has been bought and sold a few times. The current owners give tours and hold Halloween events with the proceeds going towards restoration. There are some plans to convert the abandoned hospital into a hotel for thrill seekers looking for paranormal activity. I can only imagine people pretending to see and hear things because they want to see and hear them. The world seems easier for some if they think something can happen after death. That makes more sense to them for some reason. Instead of living in the world we know, they're hoping to live in a non-world we don't know. This hotel idea is merely a plan to exploit others. I recall the 1988 movie "High Spirits" when the owner of a dilapidated Irish castle, in order to gain tourist revenue, decides to fake hauntings to attract the attention of paranormal thrill seekers only to have it backfire by a real haunting taking place. Shenanigans ensue, and there's a happy ending complete with Darryl Hannah, Peter O'Toole, Beverly D'Angelo and none other than Steve Guttenberg.

Waverly Hills is called anything from the most haunted place in the eastern part of the United States to one of the most haunted places in the world. All places have an equal amount of haunting if by haunting one means populated by the spirits of dead people, but the myth of Waverly Hills continues to develop with the growing interest of ghost-hunting reality TV shows and horror movies. My point of view regarding ghosts has always been the same. If I can't impact a thing, then that thing can't impact me. If I can't hurt it, then it can't hurt me.

The year I lived in Louisville, I was around fourteen years old, and I didn't live very far from Waverly. People in school would talk about it, so a few friends and I decided to go. They'd been before, but I hadn't. When we went, my buddies picked me up in the subdivision I lived in. We drove down The Outer Loop to 3rd Street and eventually crossed Dixie Highway and parked the car in a Burlington Coat Factory and Target parking lot. We walked the rest of the way, some on the roads until we got closer, then into the woods to not get caught. It's quite a walk up the hill to get to Waverly.

We went in the winter, February maybe. I remember not being scared. I also remember thinking, "I'm glad we came here during the day" because had it been night, I'm sure my imagination would have run wild there.

Due to all the stories and urban legends surrounding the hospital with the "body chute/death tunnel" and all, it became quite common for teens in the area to break into the abandoned hospital to see what's inside. The year I lived in Louisville when my friends and I broke in, there wasn't much to see. It's spooky because of knowing what went on there, but it was a rundown and neglected hospital with graffiti and broken windows and garbage strewn everywhere. The rooms I went in were empty. The only "scary" things we saw were the things we fabricated with our own thoughts.

We went in during the day. I've never been there at night, and I'm sure being there at night would make it much scarier. The so-called "body chute" is a tunnel that was built to receive supplies, give an entrance to the employees, and remove the deceased without being so out in the open. It goes from the main building to the bottom of the hill. It's a few hundred feet long. It's a ramp accompanied by steps, one side for walking to and from the building, the other for bringing in supplies and taking the deceased out on gurneys. The dead were taken this route, so the patients wouldn't see the bodies going which would bring down morale. My friends and I didn't stay very long.

I don't know if teens still go to Waverly. When I was young, it was quite the thing to do. Some kids went there to hang out, smoke pot and vandalize. Some went there to just see the place out of curiosity like my friends and I did, and some went to make out and have sex. Now that the place is on TV all the time, I bet it's a little more guarded. In 2006, a movie titled "Death Tunnel" was released which was filmed at Waverly Hills, and the documentary "Spooked" was also filmed there which was released the same year.

At one point, an investor was going to turn it into a minimum-security prison. At another point, the world's largest statue of Jesus was going to be erected there.

In the fifteen months my uncle Junie was in Waverly, he escaped more times than he can remember, and he had two surgeries for TB. It was during one of his escapes that his wife got pregnant. Why not escape a hospital when you have TB, right? It's only a highly contagious disease, and Louisville was suffering from an outbreak.

My grandma said, "We'd all just be sitting around in the evening, and then the phone would ring. It'd be Junie asking Jim to come pick him up somewhere. Of course, Jim would go get him." Jim was my grandfather. When I asked her what they all thought of him escaping while he had TB, she merely shrugged it off. None of them got it. It would be quite challenging to stay away all that time while your wife and family aren't with you, especially while your wife is pregnant.

In pop culture, Waverly is considered one of the most haunted places in the world. There are television shows, documentaries and books all about Waverly and what went on there. People speak of it in hushed tones due to the exaggerated number of deaths that supposedly occurred in the hospital.

When Uncle Junie talks about it, which isn't that often, that's not the image he gives. He doesn't deny lots of people dying. He doesn't talk about it much either. He does talk about learning to play the guitar while there. He also talks about making jewelry boxes out of matchsticks. He'd strike a match, blow it out, and then use it to decorate jewelry boxes. He also made small hand-tied doilies for family members. These things are still kept in the family.

My grandmother has one of the matchbox jewelry boxes. I've seen it. The tiny struck matchsticks glued together make a wood veneer for a cigar box. They're quite interesting. The doilies are odd in the sense that Junie isn't the kind of man I imagine making doilies. He's undoubtedly a product of his generation. Men were men, and women were women. There were strict gender roles back then. The doilies simply don't fit him. That's probably why I'm as fascinated with them as I am.

When I asked Junie about the doilies and matchstick jewelry boxes, he said, "I needed somethin' to do. I was in there for a long time, and time spent away from your family always feels longer than it actually is. We had crafts to occupy ourselves. I made things to give to people like your Nanny. I'd make 'em and give 'em away. That's it. Making those was just somethin' to do." My grandmother goes by Nanny to her grandchildren. Uncle Junie is her brother. I can't imagine sitting around waiting all that time while my family was on the outside living life without me while many around me were steadily dying from the exact disease I have. It seems awful. Keeping in mind the absence of cable TV and the internet, making matchstick jewelry boxes and doilies seems a good option to occupy thought to me.

He says he can't even remember how many times he escaped. It's not a good story overall, but it is a romantic story. Junie was desperate to see his wife and children. Imagine being locked away from your family when you're twenty-two years old. It had to be torture. His wife had to raise their family while he was in the hospital. No one is going to say breaking out of the hospital was a good thing while he had this very contagious disease, but we can understand the situation. I'd like to say I'd have done the same thing.

Junie told me it wasn't difficult to escape. As the nurses and staff would leave the room in the evenings, he'd shove a folded up matchbox in the door keeping it from locking. Then he'd sneak out.

Once he made it to the door, they couldn't catch him. He says, "Fast like a rabbit! That's me, the Rabbit of Waverly Hills!"

The memories of those dying around him must be challenging to think about. It would be something I'd not like to discuss. I didn't want to press him on any specific aspect. I took the stories he gave me and wrote them down. If he didn't want to talk about it, I didn't badger him. When he'd escape, he'd get home, spend some time with his family and then go back. Junie was a lucky one. He lived.

The Rabbit

The First Night

My first night there, after they dropped me off, this was late August or early September, the room they put me in was all the way at the end of a hall, no one around. When the person who showed me to the room left, I noticed the door. You see, the doors all opened into the rooms and locked from the outside. I knew if I put something in that door, it wouldn't shut all the way and lock, so I folded a book of matches for the next time someone came in.

The guys I met that day were trying to cheer me up and talked me into taking a chance on Friday Night Fights. Friday Night Fights was a pretty popular thing back then. People bet on them with chances. You'd pick a boxer and a round. I wasn't really into it, so just to get rid of 'em, I picked a boxer and a round and gave 'em a dollar. As they left, I shoved that book of matches in the door, so that it wouldn't shut and lock. It worked. I was gone.

I kept to the trees and bushes. I didn't want to run down the road 'cause they'd see me, but the guys, the other patients, they saw me. There were trees and bushes, and man, it was all downhill! Waverly's up a big hill, ya see, and there was a big ditch at one point, maybe six feet wide. I ain't never been much of a jumper, but I had so much speed and momentum goin' down that hill, I cleared that ditch in one jump! That's how I got the name Rabbit

That first night when I got away, I called my brother-in-law Jimmy to come and get me. Well, Bonnie, my wife, was stayin' at her parents, and they wouldn't let me there 'cause TB is contagious. Jimmy and I went and got her, and she and I walked up and down Portland Avenue. When we got back to Jimmy and Bill's house (Billie is Jimmy's wife and Junie's sister), Bonnie's parents called sayin' the hospital called and said they'd call the police if I didn't come back, so Jim took me back the next mornin'.

Friends and Enemies

My buddies there were Albert, Wesley and Harold. We had a quartet. I played the guitar. This one doctor, he hated me, and I hated him right back. I called him Roach because I hated him, and his name was Broach. I can't remember his first name, but he tried to stop me from having my guitar there. Albert was a lawyer. Albert was running his business from the hospital. Well, Albert told me there was no way they could stop me from havin' my guitar. Roach hated me because of my guitar. He called it my banjo. 'You'll see! You can't keep that banjo here! You'll see, Christian!' Yeah, we did see. I kept my guitar the whole time.

I never liked that Roach. He never called me by my name either. He called me Christian, my last name, never by my first name. I hated that guy. He even tried to put a stop to us makin' things. I never understood that boy.

We were all just lookin' for ways to pass the time, right, and he didn't want nobody doin' nothing! I just didn't understand it. I mean, none of us wanted to die, but for most of us, we felt like we were just there sittin' 'round waitin' to die, and he didn't want us passin' the time with nothin'. He was just a sorely kinda person. He committed suicide later on. I've always wondered if I had anything to do with that, callin' him Roach all that time like I did. He was so mean to us. Most of the people who died were old men. The younger ones like me, we didn't die.

The rest of the staff out there loved me 'cause I made things, with my hands, ya know. I made all kinds of things out there passin' the time. I made jewelry boxes out of matchsticks. I could put patterns on 'em like rattlesnake patterns. I made doilies, too. I even got to where I was makin' those balls for bedspreads people had back then, popcorn chenille. I think that's what you call it. I only made one of those, but I gave it to nurse Hattie. Nurse Hattie and I were thick, man. She was a big-butted woman, and we were thick as thieves. I sure did get along well with her. She was real good to me. She was a real good person to all of us.

Most of the people who were there lost their jobs. That'd be all over the news if that kinda thing happened these days, but back then, it didn't mean nothin'. Things were really different back then compared to today. People seemed to care more for each other, but businesses seemed to care less for people even their own employees. If you lost your job, the hospital could give you a job workin' there. They'd pay you, and you could keep livin' there. A couple good friends of mine met there and even got married there. Both of 'em had severe cancers. They'd both lost large parts of their faces to cancer.

Cancer. The way I've got it figured, those of us that made it through all died of cancer. Nine out of ten of us did anyway. That's the way I've got it figured. When I read in the paper of one of us dyin', we always die of cancer it seems. The only one left other than me is Wesley. He became a dancer, wins awards and travels the world dancin'. He likes to fish for those peacock bass in Brazil. I haven't talked to him in over two years. Maybe he's dead now, too, for all I know.

Meds and Chess

While you're there, you're on three medicines, right: streptomycin, PAS and INH. I can't remember what those letters stand for, but after your surgery, you have to keep takin' those two. They shrink the scars down, so the doctors can operate. Well, after my operation, I got a pass to go home for Christmas. I told Hattie, "Please get all the PAS and INH you can, cause I ain't comin' back!

I'll get a doctor on the outside. I gotta be with my wife and kids!"

Hattie did. She got me all she could. I got that stuff out and never went back. I never did find a doctor, but I kept taking the INH and PAS.

After my first surgery, they moved me to a new floor. My new roommate was Louie, and my new doctor was Larry. I can't remember his last name, but his first name was Larry. You know, there are good doctors and low down doctors. Larry was one of the best, and Roach was the lowest down. Larry taught me and Louie how to play chess. You know what, once he taught us to play, he couldn't beat us! He never did! I can't believe that! He'd walk in a say, "Junie, I got time to play a game of chess. Wanna play?" I'd play, ya know. What else was I doin'? Once he could tell he wasn't gonna win, he'd start gettin' a nervous leg and bouncing it up and down. He'd get so frustrated that he'd pretend to accidentally bump the table messin' up the game, or he'd say, "Oh, I'm running late. We'll have to play another time."

I Was Always Into Somethin'

There weren't no record players or nothin' out there. A friend of mine got some magazines, not dirty magazines just regular ones, and in one of those, I found a company selling records and record players. None of us had any money, and the hospital wasn't gonna spend no money, so I wrote 'em a letter. I told 'em where I was, what I had and that most of us out there weren't expected to live. I asked 'em if they'd send me a player and some records. You know what, days later, I got a player and five boxes, enough to fill a hand dolly, full of records, hit songs, too! I remember one of 'em was that song "My Ding-a-Ling." That's funny! They kept sending records, too. The staff started gettin' upset because we got so many of 'em!

Another fella out there named Hatfield, a nice guy but a little slow. Well, we made good sport of him. When he heard how we got them records, he asked if he could send a letter of his own. I told him to copy mine if he wanted, and he did. Well, they sent them records again. Well, Albert was a lawyer, and he told us he had a plan to scare Hatfield. You know, just scare him for fun. He wrote up a legal sounding letter accusing Hatfield of fraud and that legal action was gonna be pursued. We put the letter in an envelope and gave it to him. He read that letter, and his face turned white as a ghost, man! He was shakin' and cryin', "Oh, Junie!

They're gonna send me to jail when I get outta here!" Man, I was always into some shit out there!

We got Hatfield good another time, too. We were all up late one night tellin' ghost stories, and Hatfield was scared of ghosts, ya see, and he didn't have a roommate. Well, we rigged up some fishin' line with a hook attached to the end. All the rooms had transom windows connectin' 'em. We attached that hook in his room through the transom window before we started tellin' ghost stories. Once he went to his room, we started messin' with that fishin' line we attached to stuff, movin' it around like. He wasn't in bed twenty minutes, and all the sudden we heard a loud thump! He was so scared he didn't even try to open the door! He just ran into it and kept runnin' into it!

The nurse come flyin' down the hallway openin' his door. She was a big woman, broad shoulders, German I think. Well, Hatfield come runnin' out his room like a bat outta hell! She had to chase him down! She went back to his room and saw what we did. She brought him back to us sayin', "Now you all feel his pulse! You see that? His heart's racin'! You guys coulda killed him! You should be ashamed of yourselves pickin' on him as you do!" I pulled all kinds of shit out there! I was always into somethin'!

My buddy Harold and I got to where we'd sneak out and go get beer. We couldn't get out our room, and the back porch went all the way across the building, but it was at least a thirty-foot drop. There weren't no goin' that way, but Albert's room was in the front. He let us go out his window if we'd bring him back a six-pack. Harold wasn't old enough to drink, but I was. We'd walk in the bar, and sometimes they'd ask for my ID. Harold looked older than me but wasn't, and back then, I looked way too young to be drinkin'. Once I'd show 'em my ID, they didn't even ask for Harold's. We'd sit there and get about half-drunk, get that six-pack for Albert and head back. Nothing better than a frosted mug full of beer.

Thoracoscopy

I see on the television that people say that place is haunted, talkin' bout all the people who died there. I don't know. When I was there, lots of people died around me, and lots of people died before I was even there. I mean, I heard back in the 50s it was really bad there, after the war and stuff. None of us ever even talked about ghosts outside of tryin' to scare each other with ghost stories like when I scared Hatfield. We never saw any ghosts.

We never saw anything weird, or, not that I know of anyway. No one talked about it anyway.

Except, well, I don't know what we saw. Ya see, when I was there, I was married, a grown man. I had a wife, and my one roommate Wesley was married, too. Well, ya see, on Sundays, because there weren't a lot of visitors on Sundays, Wesley and I would take turns giving the other one privacy. My wife got pregnant while I was there if you know what I mean. One week, Wesley and his wife would go for a walk while Bonnie and I could have the room. The next week, Bonnie and I would go for a walk givin' them privacy.

This one time, I remembered there was a floor I'd not been on. Well, I talked Bonnie into goin'. We got to the elevator, and she tried to stop me, "You're going to get in trouble. Now let's not do this, Junie." Damn, I was always in trouble for something out there. Anyway, I talked her into it. We got off the elevator and walked in this big room. It was empty except gurneys that had sheets around 'em. I said, "Hey, there ain't nobody here! Let's get on one of these", so there I was, tryin' to get her to fool around on one of these gurneys. She glanced over and started screamin'! I didn't know what was goin' on! I said, "What? What's goin' on?

What's happenin'?" She said, "We're in the morgue! There's bodies over there!" I looked over, and there was somethin' on one of those gurneys. It looked like a head. We got the hell outta there. I told the others about it. Hattie, the nurse, said there weren't no bodies on that floor. Nobody believed us. I don't know what I saw. It coulda been a body or equipment, but whatever it was, it sure scared the hell outta us.

That's not to say things weren't scary there. There weren't no ghosts I ever saw, but we saw and endured a lot of scary things. One of the scariest things we had to go through was the thoracoscopy. It's a terrifyin' thing especially when someone tells you about right before you gotta have it done.

See, here's how it works. They strap you into a chair, your arms and legs are strapped down, and the chair's attached to the floor. They tilt your head way back as far as it can go, and people hold you still. They blindfold you. They said it's to keep stuff outta your eyes, but I think it was to keep us from being even more scared than we already were. Then, once they got your head all the way back, they'd stick a long stainless steel pipe down your throat to your lung or stomach or whatever they're lookin' at. Once the pipe is down, they stick an even smaller one down that pipe with a small mirror on the end to look for the scar in your lung from the TB. It was hard as hell not to cough with that down your throat, and those guys are holdin' your head. It was awful, but once we'd had it done, it became our job to scare the new ones tellin' 'em about it before they had to go and get it done.

I remember this one guy, big strong black guy. He was about to go in, so I started tellin' him all about it. He got so scared and got ta shakin'. He wasn't even in twenty minutes and Dr. Ransdell, he's the doctor who did most everything out there and did it all pro bono, come out that room, "Goddammit! That fella is the most terrified and screamingest person we've had in there! I'm gonna to have to knock him out! He tore the chair outta the ground!" I laughed and laughed thinking about that fella rippin' that chair outta the ground 'cause he was terrified. He didn't break the arm straps. He tore that damn chair outta the ground!

Like I said, they're looking for the scars. What happens is, TB makes scars, and then they rupture. That's what makes blood come out when you get to coughin'. If the scar is near the top, you're better off. Mine was at the very top. Albert, my buddy, his was near the bottom. He had all kinds of problems. They had it much worse when it was on the bottom. They didn't make it most the time.

Sometimes, outta nowhere, one of these guys would decide to up and die, and that's when it was bad. See, Hattie, the nurse, well, she was the 3rd shift nurse. She didn't have nobody with her at night. Well, one of these guys would up and start having fits. She'd yell for me and Wesley cause we were always awake, and she knew she could count on us. We had our hobbies, and I even had a TV, so we were always up. She'd start ta yellin' , "Junie, Wesley, get in here! I need ya!" We knew immediately to grab a bucket of ice, both of us did. See, you gotta have crushed ice around at all times for this stuff. When people'd hemorrhage, that blood starts ta squirtin' up out their mouths with each breath and heartbeat. That blood can squirt up a foot even. You start packing that crushed ice in tryin' to fill that cavity. It never worked. Not one time that it happened did they live. They all died, and we'd clean the blood off us and the floor. It was bad. I was there fifteen months. You never knew if you were gonna come outta there alive. I didn't know.

*****

I could tell the ones who weren't gonna make it. I don't know how, but I could just tell, something in their eyes or how they acted. I knew right away if they'd make it or not. It was sad to meet them knowing they wouldn't make it. It was also sad when they passed. I bought my '49 Ford from my first roommate. He died. My second roommate died, too. It was a difficult time. I had two operations while I was there. It was tough, but I made it. Many didn't. That was tough, you know, seeing them people I got to know die from the same thing I had, and I didn't. I don't think I had more to live for than they did. I just was lucky.

Eugene Johnson: Tomahawk Man

Eugene Johnson is a "poet". He showed up every Tuesday for an open mic at the neighborhood bar Zazoo's in the Crescent Hill neighborhood of Louisville, KY. It's long since closed and is now a restaurant, but it's where I tested new material. You see, I perform amateur stand-up comedy as a hobby. Eugene also performed at this open mic as it wasn't just for comics. It was for all kinds of performers. He wrote and performed what he called poetry. I performed comedy. I've never cared if I make audience members laugh. I prefer to write jokes that make other comics laugh. If a joke can make other comics laugh, it's a good joke. I often think of the old line by W.C. Fields, "If you want to make people laugh, tell a joke about an old lady falling down a flight of stairs, but if you want to make comics laugh, push an old lady down a flight of stairs." At least I've always been told that's W.C. Fields.

I primarily perform comedy at open mics. An open mic is a show that lets comics test new material and work on older stuff they've not quite got right. I prefer these shows to most other shows. Not all open mics are just for comedy; some have musical acts and poetry readings. Poetry and comedy, in my experience, don't mix well. Most comics don't respect poetry, most likely from lack of background and understanding, and, therefore, end up making fun of most poets unless it's a cute woman, then they'll pay attention regardless of the quality of the poetry. Also, lots of writers who show up to open mics to read their poems aren't, honestly, the best writers in town. Many of them have thin skin, and open mic comics are often jerks.

I first started performing at open mics in the small neighborhood bar Kazoo's once a week. The host Divinity did an excellent job of keeping the heckling of the poets down, or at least, she got most of them to do it out of earshot. Eugene Johnson was one of the poets who regularly showed up and performed. What bugged me the most is he went by the nickname "Tomahawk Man".

First, it's an obvious nod to Edgar Allen Poe. Poe was sometimes called "Tomahawk Man" while he was a critic because he was quite harsh. Personally, I've never read any of Poe's criticisms. I've just read the reports that Poe was a mean critic. I can understand that. Poe is a fantastic writer and one of my favorites. This made me immediately dislike Eugene. How could someone compare her or himself to such a great writer, such a great creative force? I've never understood self-imposed comparisons. Such comparisons are disgusting forms of vanity.

Eugene was a tall, slender man, somewhat gangly, almost how I picture Ichabod Crane from "The Legend of Sleepy Hollow" but perhaps not quite that tall and lanky. Eugene kept to himself as most of the poets tend to do unless they talk with each other. They rarely speak to the comics. I have a great deal of respect for poetry and anyone brave enough to write their own and recite it in a room full of people knowing a significant portion of them, the comics, are actively making jokes about you and your work. Comics like to talk about how difficult performing comedy is. I know very few of them who've even tried to read a poem much less write one and read it in front of people.

Eugene, like me, showed up early to the bar for that open mic. Both of us arrived about an hour early and would order food from the kitchen. We'd speak occasionally. Even when he'd initiate, he'd still be quiet and somewhat standoffish. He wore a brown fedora with an oversized brim, and when it was cool enough outside, he wore a dark brown pea coat. He seemed a fairly pleasant guy. I can't recall a single conversation we had. Eugene was friendly, but his poetry was awful.

For months I watched Eugene take the stage as "Tomahawk Man" and read his poorly written "poetry." Tomahawk Man calls it "poetry", but in fact, it's not poetry at all. It's prose. There are little to no poetic rules being followed. In fact, it lacks any noticeable rule. Therefore, this makes it not poetry. It's prose. We could call these prose poems perhaps, but they weren't even that. Their imagery was shallow and immature. There wasn't any rhythm, or if there was, Eugene simply couldn't recite it with any. If these poems had intensity in them, they weren't read with any. They lacked any semblance of anything poetic. If we are to call it "free verse" poetry, then are we talking about poetry? It reminds me of Kerouac claiming to write "American Haiku" which don't follow the rules of haikus, thus making them not haikus at all.

Oh, what's the big deal, right? It's poetry. No, it is a big deal, and here's an example to illustrate. Imagine watching people on a stage. They are jumping, twisting, running, sometimes in rhythm with each other, sometimes not in rhythm with each other. Now, imagine that one of the central items is a ball. At first, it would be easy to call what I described as a dance. When I added the ball, it is easy to call it a sport, but which one? Is it basketball or football or soccer? It doesn't matter. It could be any of those. The point is, all these things share commonalities, but they are different things that follow different rules. Poetry has specific rules that need to be followed for it to be poetry. Without those rules, it is prose.

Tomahawk Man, despite attempting to appear well-read with regards to literature by using an obscure reference to Poe, should know those rules if he is well-read with regards to literature especially if he's going to reference himself to a famous writer like Poe. In my view, this showed little to no intellectual integrity on the part of Eugene Johnson.

Eugene's poetry sounded like the ramblings of a teenage girl. He didn't even seem connected to the words he said, the words he'd written. He stumbled over and misread them often not making sense because of misreads, and seemed to be reading the words of another person. Before each reading, he'd play a little recorder, the plastic children's instrument from elementary school. He actually had one of those. He'd play a small piece before he began reading, between each "poem" and when he ended his set. He was not good at playing it, and he stumbled across the recorder worse than his words.

Typically when Eugene would take the stage, people would walk away. They'd go to the bar and order a drink or go outside to smoke. Oddly enough, I'd sit and listen to his poorly written prose. Why? I have no idea. I recall many evenings when I would be the only person left in the room while he read. This often made me feel a bit bad for him, and sometimes, I'd even be making sport of him via text message to people who weren't with me.

Time passed as it does. Months and months went by. I didn't go back to Zazoo's for Divinity's open mic for almost a year. At the end of the night, after I did my act and most others performed whatever it was they were performing, I realized Tomahawk Man never took the stage. I asked Divinity, who was a friend to everyone who showed up, where Tomahawk Man was. She told me that Eugene stopped coming in a few weeks prior. Nobody seemed even to notice he wasn't there anymore. She also said he was very private, and no one knew much about him.

Time passed by again, and months later upon my return to the bar for the open mic, there was still no Tomahawk Man. It reminded me of the first time I met Eugene Johnson and thought he looked like Ichabod Crane. Not only did he resemble the physical description, both men just disappeared. With Tomahawk Man, not even a crushed jack-o-lantern was left as evidence.

A little while later, I was reading the newspaper, something I rarely do. I noticed in the obituaries that Eugene Johnson passed away. He was not survived by anyone. It wasn't that he was not married and without kids. It is quite the opposite. He was at one point married and had a daughter. You see, Eugene "Tomahawk Man" Johnson committed suicide. He was struggling with the death of his daughter and wife at the hands of a drunk driver. They were killed on Father's Day. They were in the car on the way to his wife's parent's house for a visit and cookout. A drunk driver crossed the interstate median on I-71, slamming head-on into them. His wife and daughter died, not on impact, but they did die at the scene. Eugene only had minor injuries. He was trying to get his wife and daughter out of the car as it was on fire. They were pinned in and unconscious. They burned to death right before his eyes. All he could do was watch their skin blacken as life was extinguished before him as people dragged him away to save his life.

I attended the service. There were not many people there. It was at the funeral home that I learned the story of his wife and daughter. I was a little saddened to see no one else from open mic attend. Suicides are always hard to deal with. I stopped to look at a picture of him and his wife. She was a beautiful woman. Her mother told me that she was about to turn forty. They were high school sweethearts.

As I looked at the flowers and other pictures and different things that were placed around the funeral parlor remembering Eugene, I noticed he was being buried with a little book. It was his book of poems. Better yet, it was his daughter's book of poems. She was seventeen when killed in that car wreck. That is why Eugene's poetry seemed like a teenage girl's poems. They were. I asked the few family members that did show up about the daughter. Apparently, she was soon to be going to The School of The Arts Institute of Chicago as an English major. She'd graduated a full year early. She received a full scholarship. The whole family was so proud and excited for her. She was an exceptional student that excelled in the arts, but her love was of poetry. Her favorite writer was Edgar Allen Poe.

Seldoon: The Haiku King

When I was thirteen, my family moved into a new house along Blue River in Harrison County, Indiana. That's southeastern Indiana, just across the Ohio River from Kentucky. I've always found it funny that people in both Kentucky and Indiana refer to the Ohio River as the widest river in the world because it separates the north from the south.   It's interesting that people in Louisville, Kentucky, do not think of themselves as living in the south while everyone else in the country does. The Mason Dixon Line separated Pennsylvania from Maryland and West Virginia, but the MidWest and the South are divided by the Ohio River.

Growing up in southeastern Indiana, I was called a "Hoosier" my entire life, and most of my young life, I was repeatedly told no one knows where the term "Hoosier" comes from. There are all kinds of silly stories concerning, "whose ear" and "who's there" and so forth, but those are absurd. Near St. Louis and along the Mississippi, "hoosier" was used as a name for "poor whites". It's also a word used in shipping that meant "to be tricky". In Indiana today, according to state information, it comes from a contractor named Samuel Hoosier. He was hired to excavate the first canal of the Falls of The Ohio River. He hired people from nearby Indiana communities along the river like New Albany. These men became known as Hoosier's Men, and thus, "Hoosiers". It's not silly or romantic, and I've always thought that's why older people didn't tell me that story growing up. I'm not sure how factual this story is, but that is the official claim by the state government. There are no records of Samuel Hoosier being paid to do this, but records weren't kept well in those days.

This was the 70s, before the internet, MTV, and video games. I didn't spend a lot of time in the house. I played outside all year around. It was more difficult to play out in the summer than the winter despite Indiana's bitterly cold winters. The summers are ridiculously humid in the Ohio Valley. The average summertime temperature in southern Indiana is 90 with an average humidity in the mornings around 85%. When it's cold, you can keep putting on layers to warm up. When it's hot and humid, there's no less clothing than naked, and someone will call the cops. We mostly swam a lot in lakes and rivers and so forth. Not too many of us had pools back then.

We didn't move far. We stayed in the same area. We moved closer to the river. We used to fish and canoe a lot. In our new place, the river was the border of our property and the county. My mom and dad drove separate cars to the neighboring town of Milltown. Then my dad would ride back with my mom. After our canoeing journey, we'd pile the canoes in the bed of my dad's truck, and then we'd all ride back to the house often stopping at a local place called The Dairy Dip for ice cream or some other cooling snack. I usually got a purple or red Slush Puppie as I've never been a fan of ice cream.

We moved into a lovely house. I had a brother and sister, and until then, my brother and I shared a room. In our new house, we all had our own rooms. My room was actually in the basement. I was older than my brother by a few years, and my sister was older than me by a couple of years. She'd only recently started driving with her learner's permit. For her sixteenth birthday, she got an old Volkswagen Beetle. I had a bad feeling that car was going to be mine in a few years when she went off to college. "Oh well," I'd say. I got most of what I wanted and needed for nothing. Actually, I wanted a Corvette and thought a Mustang was a nice compromise. Little did I know I'd get a used Volkswagen Rabbit. It was powder blue. It had four doors, and only one of them opened from the outside. It was diesel and smelled awful. It got great mileage, but no one cared about mileage back in the late 80s when I started driving. It won no races and the attention it did receive, well, it wasn't what I'd have received with a Mustang or Corvette.

Looking back on that time, I'd say Mark Twain would have been proud of me. I spent a lot of time in the woods roaming the countryside in search of ponds and barns and old abandoned houses and the occasional cemetery. One of my favorite adventures was to walk in the easements of the giant power lines nearby. Even before moving to that property, my friends and I were already suspects in many blackberry heists. Blackberries are like gold in the summer. People prize their favorite blackberry patches. We knew them all and would plunder them one by one throughout the season. We'd gather them up in small buckets and then hideout in nearby barns. We were never caught and were always suspected.

One beautiful day, I was walking through the woods on my way towards a blueberry patch I'd frequent. Blueberries aren't common in Indiana like blackberries. That didn't matter much as I preferred blackberries, but this day, I'd decided on blueberries. I was on my way to the meeting point with my buddy Jason. We were going to meet at the "tire tree" at river and cross there, past the abandoned cemetery in the woods and up to the blueberry field from the backside. I'd not known Jason long as he lived just across the river in the neighboring county, so we didn't go to school together, but we had a lot in common including pilfering berries and fruits and corn from farmers. Indiana grows delicious white corn if you can find the right field. Farmers there also produce a lot of popcorn which isn't tasty at all unless popped and coated with butter and salt.

After I met up with Jason and we started towards the blueberries, we came across a strange man in the woods. We all spotted each other at the same time, so Jason and I got real quiet. He was walking towards us. He had long hair and a beard. His clothes were tattered, and he walked with his head down. As we passed by each other, he nodded at us, and Jason said, "hi" as we walked by.

This caught me off guard. All the time I'd spent in this countryside, I'd not encountered an adult in our kid kingdom. I asked Jason, "Who was that?" Jason said, "Oh, that's the weird guy who lives out here somewhere. He's come to our house a couple of times in the winter asking for food and stuff. He's harmless. My folks tell me not to worry about him. They say he's a poet. He lives alone without electricity and stuff. I've seen him fishing a couple of times, and he's allowed to take eggs from our chicken coop when he needs them. My dad said they went to church together when they were kids. His name is Wade, but he goes by a different name. I can't remember what it is. He did show me a great fishing hole in the river once. I caught the nicest smallmouth bass there."

All this baffled me. The rest of the day, I questioned Jason regarding the guy in the woods. Jason didn't know a lot other than what his parents told him which wasn't much. All he knew is that something happened to this man, and he ended up living alone out in the woods somewhere.

When I got home with my spoils which Mom scolded me for taking while she ate them, I told her and Dad about the man in the woods. My parents found it very unsettling that an adult man was living out there somewhere. Immediately, my dad called Jason's parents to find out more. Jason's dad said that there wasn't much to worry about. The man in the woods didn't steal, and if he needed or wanted something, he'd come and ask before he'd take anything, and since we lived on the other side of the river, he more than likely wouldn't bother us at all. He tended to stay on that side. None of that made my dad feel any better.

Jason's dad, to make my dad feel better, invited my dad to meet the man in the woods. Jason's dad knew where the guy lived and would find him and see if he could arrange a meeting.

Jason and I were not allowed to go to the meeting with the man from the woods. When my dad got home, here's what he told me:

The man in the woods is a writer who prefers to be alone. He's not comfortable around people and is harmless. He's not as old as he looks due to how he lives. Long hair and beards age people. He was married but isn't anymore. Not many know exactly where he lives, but he doesn't steal from anyone. He only hunts, fishes and asks for everything else he needs. Somewhere out in the woods, there's a small log cabin. Jason's dad has been there and says he's not sure whose property it's on. In fact, it may belong to the state. You don't need to be afraid of him. He's quite nice and mannerly. His name is Seldoon, or, that's the name he wants people to call him. He lives out in the woods and writes. Most people in this immediate area know him and let him stay. He told me he doesn't like crossing the river, so, more than likely, we won't see him on our side. He knows the sheriff in that county, and from what Mark told me, the sheriff over there allows this to happen. The sheriff knows where the cabin is, and occasionally checks on Seldoon to see if everything is okay.

Mark is Jason's dad. I always liked him. He was a better fisherman than my dad, and he showed Jason and I a lot of tricks and tips about fishing. My dad wasn't an outdoorsman, but he liked to think of himself as one. By sixteen, I was already more of an outdoorsman than my dad. He spent too many hours of his day sitting at a desk in an office. My mom was a stay-at-home mom. This, of course, was part of why my dad was initially worried. We're a family out in the woods with very few neighbors who lived rather far away from each other. A mom, home alone all day with kids, can be easy targets for the criminally minded. My dad's worries eased once he met and spoke with Seldoon. My dad also called the sheriff later that night to confirm Seldoon's story.

The sheriff told my dad he could legally remove Seldoon if it were that big of a problem for him since he wasn't legally allowed to live there. Even the sheriff wasn't sure exactly whose property Seldoon was staying on. After speaking with Mark and the sheriff, my dad wasn't too worried, which worked out because, after that first meeting, I never saw Seldoon again.

I looked and looked for his house. I didn't even know where he lived other than the other side of Blue River, the Washington County side. Jason didn't know where he lived either. By the time I was seventeen, I'd given up looking, but I was always intrigued by the story of this hermit, monk poet.

Once I got to college, I began a lifelong appreciation for poetry. I even minored in it to go along with my BS degree in chemistry at Purdue University. I felt it made my education well-rounded to have that humanities influence. I once told one of my writing professors about Seldoon, and he said, "It'd be interesting to read his work." For years I wanted to read his work, and I realized I never would.

By the late 90s, I'd moved away from the area. My mother called, informing me that Jason's father Mark, passed away. I'd not seen him since I left for college. Jason stayed on the farm growing tobacco, which, eventually, evolved into farming soybean. This was a typical switch in the 90s in Indiana. I didn't move too far. I wanted to pay my respects to Jason and his family. Neither my brother nor sister showed up, but that wasn't a surprise as they didn't know Mark or Jason other than through me, but my mom and dad both went to the funeral home service with me. My wife and child stayed home.

A day or two after the funeral, I stopped by Jason's place to visit with him a bit. We'd stayed in contact even before social media became so pervasive, so it wasn't as if we had years of catching up to do. We chatted and ended up going out to dinner. We stopped at a local bar, which also served food, greasy burgers and soggy fries and so forth. Greasy spoons are the staff of life.

We ended up spending the entire evening remembering when and being nostalgic for our golden days of adventure in the countryside. After a while, I asked him whatever happened to Seldoon.

Jason started laughing a bit and said, "Oh, you mean Wade?"

I laughed a bit at that. I said, "Yeah, whatever happened to Seldoon, I mean, Wade the poet? Does he ever appear anymore? I never saw him again after that one time we saw him."

Jason said, "Yeah, I saw him a lot more after you went to college. I guess times got harder for him. He started asking for more and more things. We were always obliging, but after a while, you know, it starts feeling like someone's taking advantage of you. He started going to other people's houses more often, too, from what I heard. Then, all the sudden, we realized we'd not heard from him anymore. He seemed to vanish completely, so my dad called the sheriff. They went to check on him. They couldn't find him. The sheriff said he didn't want to disturb anything because he may have simply not been home and was out in the wilderness. They went back one more time, and it was the same. Wade wasn't home."

Jason went on a bit more. Seldoon went from local tall-tale and myth to local joke. The more often he went to people's houses to ask for things, the more he began getting turned away, until finally, people stopped seeing him altogether. It'd been quite a few years since anyone seen or heard from him. Another issue was now that Jason's father passed away, no one knew where he lived as the sheriff who knew him passed away, too. He'd been retired for a while anyway.

Jason told me he knew about where Seldoon lived. He surmised through things he'd heard from his dad that Seldoon was living in an abandoned rock quarry. Jason and I knew the place, but it was far, and we'd only gone one time. I do not recall seeing any signs of someone living in there. Jason said he thought Seldoon might have been living in a small cabin deep in the crescent moon cutout near the entries to the mines. He suggested that he and I look. This, of course, made perfect sense to me. I'd not done anything adventurous in years, and I'm sure it was an excellent way to get things off Jason's mind.

The next morning, Jason and I set out to find Seldoon's cabin, assuming it was in the abandoned rock quarry. As far as rock quarries go, this one was exceptionally boring, as it had no pools in it. Often, rock quarries will have nice swimming holes due to massive holes being dug and then filling up with water. Not this one. It was just a crescent-shaped hole dug out of the side of a big hill. The road leading to it wasn't even a road anymore. When we were kids, we could see the remnants of a road. Now, it was a forest with a bit of a depressed area they could be mistaken as once being a road.

It was pretty deep in the woods. I was glad we left early and took a lunch with us. We made it to the quarry. I don't know if you'd call it a quarry anymore. The entrance was grown up with trees and rocks had fallen in, pretty much blocking the entry. We had to climb over.

We eventually found Seldoon's cabin. It was near the entrance to the old quarry caves deep inside the crescent cut out of the hill just as Jason suspected. No one had been there in years. Did Seldoon move away, or did he pass away? We walked into one of the caves and found where he stored some things. It appeared he'd also been using this cave as a shelter in the winter. We saw where he'd build his fires. He'd scratched on some of the walls, too, with crude drawings.

Then it hit me. Maybe we could gather something about him if he left his poetry around. We went in the cabin, and sure enough, piles and piles of journals he'd been writing in for years. Jason confirmed that Wade would sometimes ask for notebooks and pencils or pens. We didn't try to read through them all as that seemed like it would take months if you had a team reading them. We looked in what appeared to be the newest looking notebooks. Nothing indicated he was leaving. He just disappeared.

As we read through some of it, Jason would chuckle a little every time I'd say Seldoon. I finally asked him about it.

He said, " You don't see it, do you?"

I said, "see what?"

He said, "Seldoon is noodles spelled backward."

Why didn't I notice that before? I couldn't stop laughing. The man changed his name to noodles backward. What kind of thing happened that would make someone change their name to noodles spelled backwards? Perhaps he simply found it funny. The name almost sounds like an evil character in a children's story until you realize it is noodles spelled backwards. Jason pointing that out to me changed everything I'd ever thought about Seldoon. I never thought about him the same way again.

As for Seldoon's poetry, it seems he had an affinity for Japanese haikus. At least three-quarters of everything he wrote was in some way a haiku. Lots were started and not finished, but they were attempts at haiku, and it was all awful. It was poorly written nonsense, and I don't mean in a good way.

A few years ago, I read somewhere that all writers write bad poetry. Bad writers publish it; good writers burn it. Jason and I built a bonfire that day with Seldoon's poems. It was the closest thing we could imagine as a proper funeral for Seldoon. When Jason wasn't around, I noticed a specific book sitting on a table by itself. For some reason, it seemed separated from the rest, not simply because it was separated from the others, but because it looked like it was left there to be found. Written with black marker on the outside in quotations were the words "Isidence Renn". It seemed a bit clever to me. I kept Isidence Renn to read later. It was full of letter changes, wordplay and number play.

Isedence Renn

By

Seldoon

Juanita Sunshine

Everyone calls her Sunny, but her name is Juanita Sunshine. Sunny suits her perfectly. Sunny is her smile. Sunny is her disposition. Sunny is her laughter. Sunny is her hair, and sunny is her skin. She recalls her life happily. She remembers it to the smallest details, long blond hair in pigtails with ribbons, yellow Easter dress with white polka dots, ruffled white sox and white patent leather shoes all in perfect places as her grandparents walked her around the yard hunting for eggs. She especially loved her grandma. She called her Nanny. She always thought that if she ever has a daughter of her own, she'll name her daughter after her grandmother.

She lived a perfect life with little to no stress or suffering. Suffering, to her, was her younger sister annoying her. She did cartwheels and rode her bicycle in the park. It had a lovely white basket on the front she'd fill with daisies she picked. She held hands with her friends and skipped down the sidewalk while singing songs.

Her family had a few houses around town, some of them she only recalls seeing once and never revisiting.

When she was nine-years-old, she stayed an entire year with her aunt and uncle. They had so many kids she could play with. She loved that year so much that it stuck with her the rest of her life. With everything in her life that was good, that year may have been the best. She swallowed that year and took nourishment from it the rest of her life.

When she turned fifteen, she fell in love, and despite the concerns of her family, even her aunt and uncle from out of town, she married her high school sweetheart by sixteen. They lived happily ever after.

At least that's how she remembers it. It's interesting how repressed memory works. Are these memories repressed, or are they replaced? There's little to no resemblance to her life as it was compared to her life as she recalls it. Sunny's her name, and it does suit her in disposition and appearance. Very little of the rest is true aside a few superficialities.

Her patent leather shoes were corrective shoes she was forced to wear as a child, and the reason she stayed in so many places is because her mother knew exactly how to take advantage of advertisements claiming "First Month's Rent Free." Her family had little to no money. She and her sister often had their dinner bought by men who wanted to date their mother. That was the deal, "You wanna take me out, you gotta buy my kid's dinner, too." I know that sounds like she had their interest in heart, but it was more about keeping protective services off her back than anything else.

Sunny did often hunt for eggs on Easter, but none were ever there. Her mom would later tell her she hadn't been good enough that year for the Easter Bunny. It was the same with Santa Claus. She found herself asking in her prayers, "How good do I have to be?" more often than a child should ask that question.

She did spend a year away from home. That part is factual. They weren't her aunt and uncle. They did have a lot of kids. She was removed from her mother's care and placed in foster care for a year. Their kids were the other foster children. Why this year is still such a great year of her life is due to the lack of neglect and abuse. The times with her foster parents are some of the best memories she has.

All she knew of her father was that he never showed up when he said he would. He would tell her and her sister he was going to come and get them and take them out to dinner. They'd sit and wait for hours, and he'd never show up. Sunny knew he had another family with other children. Why did they get a daddy? Did their mommy beat them, too?

After she returned to her mother, nothing changed. She endured more of the same as before until she moved out which is somewhat similar to her memory of it. She did meet her husband when she was fifteen. They married by the time she was sixteen, and she had a child by the time she was seventeen. She had a son, not a daughter. This marriage wasn't a happily-ever-after story. They divorced by the time she was eighteen.

Sunny worked hard moving from apartment to apartment, sometimes staying with friends. She kept working trying her best to care for her son, the opposite to how her mother never cared for her.

They didn't have a lot of money, but they did have a few things they liked doing together. Every Saturday, she'd take him to lunch at Big Boy restaurant. Even though he was young, he loved their food. She'd order chili and put a little tartar sauce in each spoonful. He smiled delight with that first bite through the end of lunch. They'd share a soda.

Sometimes she'd take him for drives in the car. There was no child's seat in the car. He sat in the front with her. They were both kids more or less. He liked when Sunny would drive near the airport. If they drove by just as a plane was landing or taking off and the aircraft went over their car, he'd stomp his tiny feet screaming and laughing and shaking his hands. Sunny would do the same because he enjoyed it so much. In their small, held-together-with-duct-tape, Volkswagen Rabbit, she'd sometimes even circle a couple of times trying to time it just so a plane could do it again.

At Christmastime, Sunny would take him to the shopping mall in the affluent part of town. They'd dress in their winter clothes, matching mittens and knit caps with a ball on top, striped with bright colors. Her son was tiny even compared to other children his age, and Sunny's a little tall for a woman. When they walked together, to hold her hand, his hand had to reach up. There they'd be, her long blond hair falling down her back and his wavy red curls coming out of his cap, both with big blue eyes as they walked around the mall looking at all the Christmas decorations.

Her son seemed to gravitate to bright colors instead of the shiny gold and silver decorations. They would come to one store and look in the windows for a few minutes. Then they'd move on to the next. After a while, they'd find themselves in the candy store on the second floor of the mall. Her son didn't have much of a sweet tooth, but he did like the colors and swirls of the giant lollipops, the lollapaloozas. He always wanted one and never finished one, but she'd get one for him. They'd walk the rest of the mall. She held his mittened hand while he held the lollipop in the other. They looked and smiled.

One of the apartments Sunny lived in with her son was an old three-story home that was converted into apartments. They lived on the 2nd floor, which entered through the back. They lived in a few places, but the significance of this apartment was that Sunny was convinced the spirit of an old woman haunted it. She'd put her son in his crib and walk away. There was a rocking chair in the room she used to rock her son until he fell asleep. She'd often hear the sound of that chair rocking on the wood floor. She walked in a couple of times and found her son standing in his crib facing the chair as if looking at someone.

Then Sunny met someone. It wasn't long after they met that they moved in together. He had children of his own, a son and a daughter. The son was a little older than Sunny's son, and the daughter was the same age as Sunny's son. It was an instant family, and this family endured for a long time.

Sunny tried to forget and replace her awful childhood. She tried her best to give her son and new kids a life she'd wished her own, but sometimes, when she would put them to bed at night and say prayers with them, she'd recall her prayers as a child. She did what she could not to get upset, but those traumatic years will be with her forever.

"Dear God, please don't let mommy hurt me anymore. My feet still hurt, and I don't think those marks are ever going to go away. Could you please send some food? Sissy and I are so hungry, and mommy's too busy to take us to Nanny's to eat. Do all little kids have to be hungry? I hope not. Oh, and please God, please don't let Papaw hurt me anymore. He makes me hurt, and it makes me not feel good. He tells me not to tell anyone, but when mommy found me crying, she made me tell her. I told her what he put in my mouth, and she said I was lucky, and it could be worse. I don't know how it could be worse."

Wouldn't it be nice if we could induce amnesia? Sunny had to carry all those traumatic experiences which were repeated until she moved away from her mother. There were many others, too, all like a disease she carried the rest of her life. They impact every single aspect of her being. She cannot make decisions without these things influencing her. Such trauma invades and penetrates us, unable to be removed. Why not repress and replace if we could? Could things be worse? Of course, they could and are, but why do we feel this need to compare one traumatic event to another? Instead of dismissing saying, "Well, it could be worse," why not acknowledge the trauma for what it is and do what we can to stop it from happening again and keep perpetuating?

What is it in us that desires to tell someone her or his experiences aren't as bad as other experiences? Why do we dismiss these things? What kind of broken psychology tells a child being molested that "it could be worse" indicating the same happened, but it was worse? What kind of broken individual allows that to happen to another child having had it happen to themselves?

We neglect the individual tree when we only look at the forest, and we overlook the forest if we only look at a individual tree. A single tree can be healthy while the rest of the wood falls into decay, and a forest can be healthy while a particular tree starves for nourishment. Choosing one to be concerned with neglects the others. Where did Sunny fit? Why was she ignored and neglected? What forest was considered healthy while she diminished? Why was she forced to endure the mysterious ways of a fickle God?

"We men are wretched things." -Achilles from Homer's "The Illiad". We are wretched, wretched things.

The Kiln

Hank lay still on the floor with no ability to move and not really understanding what was going on. All he could do was look around the room. He'd never been in this room before. He wasn't quite sure where he was. He didn't drive. He was too intoxicated. What he knew was that her last words to him were very unsettling, "You're not going anywhere. I'll be back in a few minutes." She pulled the shoulder length blonde wig off her head revealing long, dark hair and disappeared out of the room.

What led Hank here? All he could remember was having a couple drinks with a really good-looking blonde he met at the bar. He'd never seen her there before. It was a neighborhood bar. He'd been going there for years and years never once seeing her there. It's not the kind of place people just show up to. It's on Humphrey Lane between Pitts Point Road and Shepherdsville Road. It's not in a place easily seen. Strangers don't know that bar's even there. It's not visible from the main road. A small wooded area blocks the view from Shepherdsville Road.

She didn't fit there at all. That's why she caught his attention. She was sitting at the bar sipping on a beer in a cute little outfit. She was small. She was cute. She was dressed well. She didn't belong in that redneck bar. She didn't even talk like everybody else. Her voice sounded like she was from Chicago or somewhere north. She smelled different, too, not like cheap perfume used to cover up cigarettes and beer. She smelled pretty, and her voice was soft.

Hank didn't even know how long he'd been in the car. She said she'd drive. They were making out in the car, and she said, "Let's go back to my place." He couldn't think of a better idea. After that, he woke up when she turned the car off. They walked into the house and started making out on the couch. She went to the kitchen to get another beer. When she came back and sat down, he didn't remember much after that. He remembered feeling dizzy. Now he found himself on the floor not being able to move. He felt awake but barely. No matter how hard he tried, he could not move.

It kind of reminded him of being on the bottom of the pile when he played football. All those bodies would get twisted and tangled and piled on top of each other. Being at the bottom of one of those piles, with all that weight on you, you can't move until they start getting up. The big difference here is he felt no weight on him. He couldn't even struggle against it. In a football pile, he could fight against it, but here, there was nothing to fight against, and he couldn't even if he wanted.

He knew he shouldn't have been in that bar. He wasn't supposed to be drinking anymore. He was being watched now that his soon-to-be ex-wife was trying to get a divorce, but that wasn't going to happen. Just like every other time she tried this, he got her back. He knew he could get her back. He wasn't even worried about it. He'd be fine, for a while. Yeah, he'd knocked her and the kid around a bit on occasion, but sometimes, people have it coming. They deserve it, just like a dog. If you don't treat them as they should be treated, then they'll think they're in charge. "My daddy taught me that, and his daddy taught him." His parents and grandparents were together until death parted them. "Worked out perfect for them. Why stray from what works?"

"I shouldn'ta let this happen," he thought. "If I get in trouble right now, I'll end up in jail for sure. Haven't been back to jail since I beat up that faggot who ruined my damn life! Had the perfect job, and they hire some faggot ta be my boss? Fuck that queer and that queer judge who sentenced me. The whole world is fucked now. Queers running everything." When Hank was thirty-one, he went to jail for two years after being found guilty of assault and battery. He'd just been fired from the one decent job he ever had because he was harassing his new boss. Two weeks after losing his job, Hank went to a bar on Bardstown Road in Louisville, Kentucky he knew his then ex-boss frequented. He waited outside for him to leave, and then beat him badly. He'd have gotten away with it had it not been for a random police car pulling around the corner into the alley where the parking lot was. "Cop had ta be a fag cop. No real cop's gonna lock me up for beatin' a faggot. A real cop woulda helped me." After a brief trial, Hank was sentenced to two years in prison.

"Goddamn prosecutor made me look stupid! Talkin' 'bout me not graduatin' school. Just 'cause you go to school don't make you smart. My daddy never went to school. He was a union man his whole life. If I hadn't flunked that drug test years ago, I'da stayed in the union, too. It's the goddamn government gettin' inta er'thang." Hank's mind was wandering in and out of consciousness. "They tried ta tack on another year for a hate crime, but I took the plea. That showed 'em."

When Hank was released, he attended Alcoholics Anonymous. He did try to straighten up. Prison was torture, and he was tortured. Being athletic and big on the outside of prison doesn't make one big and athletic in prison. He had no intention of going back. That's when he met Pam. She was volunteering in the church where they held the meetings. "She was different back then, sweet and stuff. Now she thinks she's smarter than me. She didn't ever go ta college."

She did graduate high school and was going to go to college, but her parents both died in a car wreck. She struggled with this for a long time. She was raised very religious. Her parents were devout people. She was intelligent. She simply never had the chance to expand her potential.

For Hank, she was perfect in the beginning. She worked, cooked, cleaned and made sure he was taken care of even though he paid no mind to whether or not she was. In the beginning, of course, he was loving and caring, and everything was great for both of them. He was trying to straighten out his life, but with his prison record, the only jobs he could find were labor positions in the service industry like dishwashing at restaurants. He tried that for a while, and despite not making much money, Pam was happy that he was simply trying.

Every Friday night, they'd go out to their favorite restaurant and then see a movie. They loved to get an enchilada dinner and a nacho platter and split them. They laughed while munching on chips and salsa. They did this for six months. It was so good that Hank and Pam were married in less than a year. He moved in with her. In less than a year, Pam was pregnant.

"That was the downfall. She got knocked up! Once that happened, I couldn't take it anymore! Had to start drinkin' again ta put up with her damn mood swings", he thought. "Started with a margarita there at the Mexican restaurant. Next thing I knew, I was back where I started!"

"Never hit her while she was pregnant. Nope, not once", he recalled. "I never hit her until after! She was off for maternity! I was still workin'! I'd come home tired from the restaurant needin' some damn sleep!" Hank was getting drunk in the restaurant before he'd go home. Pam knew it. She tried talking to him, asking him to stop. He'd deny having a problem. She knew it was going too far when he completely stopped going to AA. One night, he came home after work, a few too many, and the baby was crying.

Hank was yelling and screaming he needed to sleep. Pam was exhausted both physically and emotionally, and she said, "Yeah, I guess you need a break from washing those plates all night while I've been here for weeks raising our child all by myself", and Hank slapped her across her face the way his daddy taught him. "Ya see, boy, when ya hit a female, ya never slap 'em in an upward motion. That might lead 'em ta thinkin' they above ya or sumthin'. Always hit 'em in a downward motion. That way they know they beneath ya like they are." Hank recalled his dad hitting him in the same manner, but that's the correct way with kids, too. That was only the first time Hank hit Pam.

She demanded he leave, but he wouldn't. He began begging and pleading. She told him to go, or she'd call the police. He was crying. She was crying, and the baby was crying. She picked up the phone and began dialing. Both knew if the police came, he was going to jail, so he left. Within a week of being alone, Pam took him back.

Things were great as they were in the beginning, and each time he hit her, they'd break up. She'd kick him out, and within a week or so, she'd take him back. Things would always be better for a little while, but that "little while" slowly got shorter and shorter. Once Hank started drinking again, he never stopped, drinking or hitting her.

Finally, he beat her up pretty badly one night. Despite being scared, the next morning, Pam sought out some counseling. Immediately, the counselor demanded Pam have Hank arrested, but Pam said she'd never testify against him. The thought of raising her child alone with their child's father in prison terrified her, so she never went back to the counselor. The counselor called attempting to follow up once or twice, but Pam never answered the phone when she saw the number.

After a few years of this, as anyone can guess, Hank hit his son in a fit of drunken anger because the boy dropped a glass on the kitchen floor. The child went flying across the floor and cut his head. He had a black eye and wound on his head at the hands of his father by age four. Perhaps Hank should have poured the drink into a plastic cup knowing children are known for dropping things, but at this point, reason and foresight were lost to Hank. After this, not only was Pam afraid for herself, she was also afraid for her son. Once again, Pam sought legal counsel.

This time, the people were a bit different. At the first meeting, the counselor, a middle-aged woman who was very nice and understanding, was primarily concerned that Pam find a safe place to stay. Pam said Hank hadn't been coming home much since he'd struck the child. After some checking, the counselor's assistant found Pam's old file. Pam told them she was quite certain Hank would not be home that night. In fact, Pam didn't see or hear from Hank ever again.

Hank was looking around the room. He had no idea how long he'd been there. He'd been reflecting on the years, trying to figure out what's got him in this position, and he's come up with nothing. There's a lot of art on the walls, "lotta crap", he thought to himself. Finally, the lady entered, pushing a red cart on the hardwood floor. She was no longer wearing the clothes she had on earlier. Her dark hair was pulled back in a tight ponytail.

"Do you recognize me yet?" she asked. "Come on, Hank, surely you can remember me if you think about it. You've been in my office a few times. I'm one of the lawyers in the prosecutor's office. I don't work on your case, but I'm well aware of it. I read the files and listen to the conversations." She paused for a moment looking at him, "You're an awful person, Hank. Do you even realize that? I bet you don't even realize that. You're a sociopath. I mean, I am, too, but you're far worse than I am."

Hank then remembered her. She's the lady who sat in the desk by the window when he'd have meetings with his lawyer and the prosecutor. He'd noticed her because he'd sometimes have to sit there waiting for a while before the two lawyers would come out of the private office. "Oh, I think you remember me. I was wondering how long it'd take. The others took about the same amount of time. You're all pretty ignorant, not stupid or dumb mind you. You're voluntarily ignorant. I can forgive a dumb person, but you, you don't have to be the way you are. You have the potential to learn. You just wish to remain ignorant. You love wallowing in your own filth."

"What I'm going to do, Hank, is tie a tourniquet around each of your limbs and then cut off every single one of them while you watch and can't do a thing about it. You know what a tourniquet is, right? It's a tight cord before a wound that slows bleeding, so you don't die," she said.

Hank's eyes must have widened. She said, "No, no one's going to find you. I've mixed just enough drugs with alcohol in your system to keep you awake but unable to move. How will I dispose of your body? It's simple. See, I'm a ceramicist. I have a kiln. Kilns get so hot that a human body is not only destroyed, but not even ash is left behind. It's hot enough to turn dirt to glass, and you're going in one cold and left there to heat up and burn. It should take about a half hour or so to heat to 970 degrees. You'll feel it. The drugs should start wearing off enough for you to feel it, but you'll be limbless and unable to do anything about it. You may live long enough to see the red glow and see your skin turn black and catch on fire, or perhaps your eyes will burn off quickly as your hair catches on fire catching the rest of your head on fire."

She rolled him over onto the hydraulic cart and raised him up a little. She began pushing him down a hallway leading out of the living room, out a patio door, down a little path through a garden and into a small building. Hank could see they were out in the middle of nowhere, surrounded by woods.

As they entered a large room, he noticed lots of ceramic bowls and cups aligned on shelves of all different kinds of colors, sizes and textures. She rolled him into the center of the room. He was on his back facing the ceiling, but he could look around. He saw her walk over to a small shelf in a dark corner in the room. She came back with a small brown burnt looking cup. She said, "This is what you're about to become. This is my first. His name was Thomas, well, Tommy to his buddies. He beat his wife and kids, too, Hank, like you do. You're all bullies. You like beating those who can't defend themselves, and it's repugnant. I have eight of these, Hank. You're about to become the ninth."

She turned his head, so he could see what she did. She walked over to a table with wheels and pushed it back towards him. There were giant pieces of long thin rubber and a reciprocating saw and scissors. She put on a protective outfit like what a painter would wear.

"You'll be one more. They're, hmmmm, trophies of sorts. It's easy. You're all easy. You men are such wretched things. I'll never be caught. I could be caught, but I highly doubt it. No one misses any of you, well, no one of importance. Yeah, your closest family members who are delusional about you may miss you, but more than likely, even your own mother would know you've nothing to offer the rest of the world aside from drunken violence and harassing women who'd rather you be hit by a bus," she said as she fiddled with the things on the table. She stopped what she was doing, looked back at Hank and said, "Actually, the only people who may miss you are others like you."

She paused for a moment looking down at the table. She looked back at him, "The trick is this. I need to throw any possible investigator way off track. This time will be as different and as the same as every other time. I pick some really far out of the way place and leave some of the personal items there, usually a wallet, jewelry or an article of clothing associated with the person like a belt buckle or something like that. For you, I'm going to get a small bucket and put a couple rocks in it. Then, on my way home from work sometime a week or two from now, I'm going to stop at the Falls of the Ohio in Jeffersonville, IN. I'll pretend to be looking for driftwood, and while bending down to pick a piece up and put in the bucket, I'll leave your wallet in the mud for someone to find. There are so many people there that one more woman collecting driftwood won't raise an eyebrow. I'll leave it in an inconspicuous location hoping it won't be found for a couple days. If it rains, all the better. It'll get washed down and wind up somewhere else even farther away."

"Some of the things I've left still haven't been found. I'm sure they will be. I try to leave them in places where it looks like they were disposed of intentionally. Of the eight so far, only six have been found. There are two still out there. The saddest aspect regarding those two, no one seems concerned those people are missing. I guess 'sad' isn't the correct word. It's obvious people don't miss people like you. I leave no traces of bodies, of course. That could lead back to me. You know, sometimes I think I don't need to leave anything to throw investigators off track. No one cares about any of you, not really. Most people who know you will be secretly happy you're gone," she said.

She cut off all his clothing with a pair of very heavy-duty fabric shears. "Look at that penis. My, Hank, is it cold in here? I thought you'd be a bit more impressive than that! Maybe you're a grower instead of a shower? Oh well, it'll never work again. Maybe I'll tie it off and remove it, too? Well, I'm not sure I can tie the rubber around it." He felt her lift his leg and tie the rubber around his thigh. She put on a headpiece with a clear plastic face shield, gloves and surgical mask. She picked up the saw and removed his leg.

He couldn't feel any pain. It was just as if someone was shaking his leg violently, but he could see blood spraying all over her. He could hear it dripping on the plastic below. His leg was gone.

After, she set the saw down, she lifted his leg and showed it to him. It was not a clean cut at all. It was jagged and torn and dripping with blood. "Here's your first appendage, Hank. Next is your other leg, and then your arms." She then proceeded to do this with every limb. She cut his arms off just below the shoulder. She showed him every limb she removed.

He knew he was limbless and lost a lot of blood. She was covered in it. She had to wipe it away from the shield covering her face quite a few times. He felt it flying all over his body. He also began feeling the pain a bit, or maybe it his mind was making it up. "It's that time, Hank. I'm going to raise your platform up and put you in the kiln", she said. She pumped the handle, and the bed began rising. "Now you're still heavy, but nothing I can't handle. I workout and weight train almost every day, so don't worry there. I won't drop you. I am going to put you in here upside down because it seems like the last bit of terrorizing I can do to you."

She rolled him to get her arms underneath his torso. He began trying to plead, but he couldn't make noise. She lifted him with a vocal straining groan. He felt his head go down, and he was lowered into the kiln head down. His neck folded as he was angled. He could feel his breathing was strained from the angle. Then she folded his legs and arms and put them around him.

It was dark and cold in the kiln, but soon it would be hot and glowing brightly. She walked away and returned with a small cup like the others. "This is you soon. It's not a true glaze, just an earth tone. I don't feel you're worth glaze. You're worth dirt because that's the only thing I can think that's beneath you. Even though none of these eight pieces are what most would call pretty, they are my favorite pieces. I'll never sell these. I'll keep these until I die," and she then set the small cup next to him.

"Guys like you are easy because guys like you are easy. Your misogyny, vanity, arrogance and stupidity have led you to believe that a woman could never get you. Even now, you can't fathom how this came to be, how you've ended up here, cut into pieces and about to die at the hands of a small woman."

She continued, "How this came to be is because you're easy in every way imaginable. All your desires are surface. There's nothing to you beyond the shell. There is no depth to you. You're the ugly candy coating. The issue is, there's nothing on the inside. There's nothing more than the coating. You're empty, and because of that emptiness, you've no value to anyone. No one will miss you. Anyone who's ever come in contact with your life's been worsened by you. Every life you are part of will be better now that you're gone. You're an awful individual, and there's no positive place for you in our world. Most of us are trying to get along and help each other. Not you, you're only concern is yourself at the expense of others. You're a parasite, and in a few minutes, you'll be gone.

I doubt you understand that you're a bad person. I don't think anyone could explain to you how your actions make you a despicable human being that you'd comprehend. I've worked in public law for years. People like you terrorize the world around them, and very little can be done. Yeah, you can go to prison, but when we remove one, it seems like ten more pop up in your place. It's a never-ending cycle of repulsion. Yes, I understand that I just said getting rid of you won't change anything, but I'm still getting rid of you," and she closed the lid.

Hank, completely unable to move and now in the darkness of a kiln felt tears swelling up in his eyes. He hoped it was a dream. Just then, a small opening in the side, a hole allowing light in, opened. As his eyes adjusted, he could make out the gruesome scene inside, pieces of himself stacked and placed around his bleeding torso. He recognized his right calf by a large freckle he'd had as long as he could remember. Then he heard her voice coming through the opening, "I'm leaving this open, so you will get a small look at yourself before the heat kills you. Perhaps you'll even get to see some of you burn." He never heard her voice again.

A moment or two later, he saw red glowing coils brighten the inside of the kiln. It was getting hot, and all he wanted to do was scream.

Backs To The Wall:
A Game For Free Spirits

On any hot day between late summer 1980 and late summer 1981, as long as it was late summer at the time, possibly very late summer as my memory is a bit sketchy on the time here, recess or P.E. would be complete, and all the students would be sweating, thirsty and in need to pee.

Waiting in line, I had to use the bathroom desperately. There was plenty of time to use the bathroom before I got in line, but oh no, that time was spent standing in line to get the biggest drink of water I could manage down my throat. It didn't occur to me that I had to use the bathroom before I drank the water. Cause and effect bear little to no consequence to such young children. The giant drink of water was now forcing its way into my "holding tank" that was already full. The pee was going to start peeing even if I didn't get into that bathroom.

As I made my way closer to the front of the line, I could hear the echoes of tons of laughter coming from inside the restroom. Hollering and cheering and laughing were the holy trinity for a young boy of my era. The pressure was building on the verge of scary. My legs were pressed together, and I'm sure my tiny body was slightly hunched while I grabbed at my crotch and dancing a pee dance. Looking around, I saw a few other little boys doing this as well. This is what I now call "necessity". Want and need have nothing to do with each other when need supersedes want which it inevitably does. Even if you want a soda, the need of hydration is what matters.

Finally, it was my turn. As I opened the door, the sight of five little six or seven-year-old boys, backs to the wall, yelling and laughing and aiming and straining… the final game of recess was in full session. "Who could pee the farthest" was in full swing.

As I waited my turn, I didn't notice the pressure on my bladder as much I did before. Who knows why that is?

The unfortunate aspect of this game is that the wall forbids one from going any farther from the urinals than the wall itself. The other (and probably most regrettable aspect) is that pee flies everywhere. Most of it did not enter the urinals. Despite the urinals being the type that went all the way to the floor, lots of pee hit the wall and floor around and the stall walls next to the urinals. I'm sure 50 percent went in the urinals. That leaves 50 percent everywhere else. With an entire first or second grade platoon of boys playing this game, we left a lot of pee on the floor and other areas in the bathroom. I hope they simply hosed the bathroom down at the end of the day.

I don't ever recall a "winner". I simply recall pushing as hard as possible and slowly backing up to the wall. The farther you got, the less pee went into the urinal. Either way, there was always a buddy standing there saying, "that's some good peein'!" which you said to him shortly before or after your turn.

Is there anyone freer than a little kid? They have no regard for the opinions of others. I was once told that freedom is wanting to obey the law. In other words, when your desires match the will of god or state or whatever you call "authority", you're free. To me, freedom is acting in a way that you simply don't care if others see or not. Freedom aligns itself with little kids. To remain this way, that is the trick. Shame and pity are for others. Acting without regard of either of these two "values" is freedom or at least a huge aspect of it.

Hamlette

In the mid to late 80s, I lived in Southern Indiana with my mom, stepsister and stepdad near the small town of Fredericksburg. Our mailing address was technically the even smaller town of Depauw, but we lived closer to Fredericksburg. We moved to this town at the end of my 3rd-grade year, but my sister and I didn't start at a new school until the following school year.

Fredericksburg is on the Blue River, which is a tributary to the Ohio River. It was both a beautiful and boring place to live. There wasn't a lot going on there, and there's even less going on there today. The last time I drove through Fredericksburg, it was barely recognizable. Most of the town is gone compared to when I lived there. Very little remains except for the dive bar, the post office and the canoe rental business. I was sad to see the old gas station with the extra cold RC machine was gone.

When we moved there, my parents were attempting to start a small farm, what most would call a weekend farm. We started with chickens. My stepdad Edward built a small chicken coop, and every day I had to feed the chickens and collect the eggs.

This wasn't a big deal. I didn't like it in the mornings before school because it was so dark and couldn't see where I was going. This place was very rural. One of the first times we visited the property after buying it, as I walked across the gravel driveway, I stepped on a copperhead's head. Edward shot the snake as they're poisonous, but I knew that dead snake wasn't the end of snakes. It was always on my young mind that I'd go into the coop and find a snake in one of the chicken roosts where the eggs were. This never happened.

We also had dogs and cats. We had over twenty acres almost entirely comprised of woods except for our yard and a small clearing for a barn we were going to build. The barn was never built, but a little shed made of cedar poles was built in the clearing. I cannot remember using the small shed for anything other than storing wood we'd cut and split that would eventually be brought to our woodshed behind our house to be used in our woodstove in the winter.

Soon after the chickens, we bought a goat. There was a surprise with the goat we purchased. The day we went to pick her up, she gave birth, so we ended up with two goats. This pleased my sister and me. I'm sure my parents weren't upset by it. The mother goat was named Lori by the farmers who sold her to us, and the kid received the name T.L. which was short for turkey legs since, according to the farmers, T.L.'s legs were a little "shaky" for a goat, even a baby goat. As a kid, I wondered if turkeys have shaky legs.

The property had a small trailer on it, which is what we lived in while our new place was being readied (a modular home). We stayed in that trailer for less than a year. It was very crowded, but I do have some pleasant memories from there. Along with the trailer, there was a pump house built on top of a cistern. There weren't water lines in this area. Folks either had wells dug or had cisterns. We eventually moved the chicken coop next to the garage and made it a little bigger. This is where the goats could go in bad weather.

I don't recall when or how, but I got a duck. It was a small duck. I don't recall my parents buying the duck. I remember there being one single duck amongst a bunch of chickens. It was a black duck, a small black duck. When I would come home from school and feed the animals, the duck would follow me around while I did my chores. Feeding the animals was my chore. My sister vacuumed and dusted. I enjoyed the company of the duck, and I spoke with it. I never named the duck. I simply called it duck. "Hi,

Duck!" I'd say as I entered the pen where all the animals stayed. The duck would make a little duck quack which has always sounded more like a "mak" to me than a "quack", and it would shake its tail feathers. They waddle. Everything about a duck is cute; their noises, walk, mannerisms, and so forth are cute, except that they poop everywhere. That's not cute. There's nothing cute about that.

Things went on this way for a while. I grew quite fond of the duck. Our daily conversations with the duck remind me of the conversations I now have with my cats.

I'd say, "Hi, Duck!"

The duck would say, "mak."

"How are you today?" I'd ask.

"Mak," the duck would respond.

I'd followup with, "that's great!"

The duck would then say, "mak" wiggling its tail feathers.

"Today at school sucked. My friend Jon and I got in trouble for making fun of this girl in English. She started making fun of us, so we started back. She got mad and told on us! The teacher then yelled at us!"

The duck said, "That teacher is such a jerk. Based on everything you've said, he's not very aware of what it means actually to be a teacher. He's simply there for summers off." Actually, the duck said, "mak," but my translation is what the duck meant.

Every single day I'd carry on a conversation with the duck in this manner. Some days the duck was more talkative than others. At first, I thought those days meant the duck was hungrier than the other days, so I'd go in the house and get a piece of bread.

This worked out only a few times. The duck did love the bread, but this received the attention of the roosters. We had four large roosters. This was a mistake, of course. We didn't mean to get four roosters, but that's what happened. I have never known which type of chicken these were, but I think they were Brahma chickens. These are big chickens with feathers stretching down their legs to their feet. I've read that Brahma chickens are usually nice, but these four roosters were not.

I tried to give the duck bread without the roosters seeing this. My plan, which worked most of the time, was to feed the chickens on one side of the pen and in their coop, and then I'd go to the other side and give the duck a torn up slice of bread. On the days the roosters saw this it became a struggle. They weren't much shorter than I was. They'd attack me, and chickens can be mean. I'd throw the bread and run away. If it would have just been one of them, I don't think it would have been an issue, but since there were four of them, it was almost as if they were teaming up on me. They'd peck and scratch me. They weren't gentle. Sadly, this led to me not feeding the duck bread very often.

After a couple of years of this, I grew too large for the chickens to bully. They'd still attack, but I wasn't scared of them anymore. I'd shove them away. They duck remained small. It never grew much.

I referred to the duck as a male, but I had no idea if it was a male or female duck. I always thought of it as a boy duck. In my mind, the duck was a boy about my age. We talked about the boy things I was concerned about: cartoons, breakdancing and any girl I thought was cute at the time. Those were the primary conversations I had with Duck.

Our neighbors had a much more extensive farm. They also had a lot of pigs. I don't know if pig farming was their primary source of income, but they had a lot of pigs and quite a few fields of corn. I also recall they grew potatoes. Their son and I were friends, and their oldest daughter and my sister were friends. She was a few years older than us, but my sister still spent quite a bit of time with her. One day, my sister came home with a piglet from the pig farm. I recall my parents not being super keen on this idea. My stepdad saying, "Pigs are different. They get massive!" My sister begged until they agreed. Of course, once the cuteness of the piglet waned after becoming a pig, my sister's interest in the pig declined as well. The pig became one more animal on our small farm. We named the pig Hamlette.

To be fair, Hamlette was often fun. She was far more intelligent than the dogs and cats. She also seemed to enjoy spending time with us. I recall one snowy day. We were sledding down our very steep and long driveway. Hamlette would run beside us as we slid down. Eventually, she did jump on the plastic sled with my sister and ride down once. I don't recall it making it all the way to the bottom, but family stories grow, becoming legend. Amongst family tales, Hamlette slid down on our sleds almost every time. I can only recall it happening once, and I'm not convinced the trip to the bottom of the hill was achieved, but the stories of Hamlette sledding with us are always a great deal of fun at family gatherings.

More than any of the other animals besides dogs and cats, the pig was accepted as a pet. We also could not keep it in the pen. Pigs are very tough. It is challenging to hurt a pig. We had Hamlette for well over a year. She grew into a full-size pig. I cannot recall the size she got, but I would have guessed she was four to five hundred pounds. My friends and I often tried to ride her like a horse. She'd bounce, throwing us easily.

Then the problems arose. The issue was simple. Hamlette was my sister's pet, but Hamlette lived with the other non-pet animals in the pen. Well, she lived there, but she didn't stay there. She was destructive and a bit of a nuisance to me. I was the kind of kid who liked to be alone quite a bit. Yes, I had a lot of friends, but often I preferred to be alone. I spent a lot of time in the woods walking, watching and listening.

I did have a couple of dogs. One was named Turbo. He was named after the character in the movie Breakin'. He was a Beagle. Turbo died, and my parents got me another dog. His name was a Bear. He was a German Shepherd and Doberman mix. I think there were other mixes to him, as he wasn't tall like a German Shepherd or Doberman. He may have weighed fifty pounds. Neither of these dogs were follow-me-around-the-countryside dogs. I was not Travis roaming the county with Old Yeller. Unlike my dogs, Hamlette the pig wanted to follow me through the woods.

Beyond following me when I wanted to be alone, Hamlette also knocked me down a lot. This wasn't a malicious act, of course. She was friendly. I was just a small kid, and she was a happy giant pig. She'd run up to me in an amicable way, bumping into me and knocking me to the ground. For over a year, almost two, I endured this. Hamlette was my daily bully without intending to be. I began dreading feeding the animals, especially when the weather was foul. She'd knock me in the mud or snow. She'd knock the food out of my hands sending me back to the pump house where we kept the food to get more to take to the chickens, goats and my duck. The fun I had with Hamlette began being substantially outweighed by the annoyances she caused me. I started to hate that pig.

Then Hamlette did something incredible. One spring day as I was watering the animals, I noticed Hamlette dug a small wallow in which to mud bathe, so I sprayed some water on it to keep it as mud. For the next couple days, when I'd get home from school and tend to the animals, I found Hamlette made the wallow larger and deeper. Each day, I'd add more water if it dried out.

Over the next couple weeks, this wallow grew into a large hole in the ground holding about a foot of water. If memory serves, I'd guess the hole three feet wide by five feet long by nearly two feet deep. As it would dry out, I'd fill it back up with water. What I got out of this the most was that the duck loved swimming in the small pool Hamlette dug.

I'd enter the pen, start filling the pool with water and the duck would come waddling, wiggling tail feathers and expressing as the duck did happily, "mak mak mak mak mak." The duck would hop into the pool as the water was raining down, swimming under the falling water. It was so much fun to watch. I looked forward to it every single day while I was at school. If I was having a bad day, I could think, "When I get home, I'll add water to the pool for the duck, and he'll love it thanking me with a 'mak mak.'" A small black duck swimming in a small pig pool brought a great deal of joy to my life. Hamlette's pool was one of the things I did like about the pig.

At the time, in my mind, Hamlette did this as a peace offering for bothering me. I mean, the pig continued to bother me, but this was the only offering I was going to get to smooth things over between us. This was the deal I assumed we made, "Look, kid, I'll dig this puddle. In exchange, I'll continue to knock you down and follow you around," a deal to which I reluctantly had to agree, a manufactured consent of sorts.

As the spring became summer and school recessed, the pool stopped growing. Once or twice I dug the pig pond out slightly deeper as mud would settle into it, making it a little too shallow for the duck to swim. Other than that, it was business as usual except a wild turkey decided to join our small farm. I was not fond of the turkey, but my stepdad was. It was a female turkey, or, at least it had no characteristics of being a male turkey.

One thing I learned from this wild turkey is that turkeys are not intelligent whatsoever. This turkey did not last long. The first winter we had with that turkey, it froze to death sitting on a tree limb during an sleet storm. Edward, saddened by the turkey's death as he liked the turkey, had to throw rocks at it to knock it out of the tree to which it was frozen. It could have gone into the coop with the goats, chickens and the duck with the heat lamp. It was much larger than the chickens except the four roosters, but they all seemed to get along.

Then one day as I went to feed the animals, the duck wasn't there. The duck didn't always appear, but most of the time the duck was there. On occasion, the duck would stay in the coop. What struck me odd was even after I began filling Hamlette's pool, the duck never showed up. That was odd. This went on for a couple of days. I looked and looked. I asked Edward, mom and sister, and no one had seen the duck. I even asked my neighbors.

Perhaps the fourth day or so, the water in the wallow was low as it was summer and dried quickly. I got the hose out and began filling it. As I was standing there, Hamlette arrived in an exceptionally happy mood pushing and shoving me kind of the way cats do with their heads to show affection. Then she shoved me so hard that I fell into the pool. This happened a couple times before, but this time, she shoved me face down onto the corpse of the duck, which was smashed into the corner of the pool having been squashed and killed by Hamlette wallowing. I began to cry. I yelled and screamed at the pig even throwing handfuls of mud at her. I remember trying to throw the still-running hose I was using to fill the pool.

Then an angry calm overtook me. My crying ceased, but my anger grew. I was staring at the pig as it looked at me sitting in the puddle, the water still spraying on me, and I was covered in pig puddle mud. I stood up, walked into the house, into my room, loaded my .22 rifle and began walking out of the house. It wasn't uncommon for me to get my .22 rifle out and shoot cans and so forth, but the context of the mud and look on my face forced Edward to stop me asking, "Where are you going with your rifle?" I responded, "I'm going to kill that pig."

"Now hold on. Wait a minute here. What's going on? I can't have you killing your sister's pig. That's not going to go over well," he said reaching out to grab the gun.

I pulled away and said, "That pig killed my duck, and so I'm going to kill it. I hate that pig, and I don't want it anymore. How is it her pet when I'm the one who feeds it? I don't like that pig, and I don't want to take care of it anymore."

He calmed me with a short talk. He took the gun away from me, and said, "Look, we know that pig is too much to keep as a pet. It was a bad idea as pigs aren't kept as pets because of their size. We're not going to have it much longer. I'm taking it this weekend when you're at your dad's house and your sister is at her mom's house. We're going to have it butchered."

Looking back on this, I don't know how I wasn't repulsed by the thought of killing a family pet much less butchering and eating it, but the moment he said it, all my anger melted away. I gave up the gun without a fight. I went back to the animal pen, washed the caked-on mud away from the duck's feathers and buried him just outside the pen.

When I returned home from my dad's house, my neighbor's, buddies of mine, told me of a grand fight between Edward and Hamlette that took place over the weekend. Pigs are big. They are muscular, and they pretty much don't do anything they don't want to do. According to family legend and confirmation from neighbors, "Hamlette's Last Stand" was fought over the course of two days, Edward losing the first day. The boys who lived across the street from me said the fight lasted hours, hours which they sat watching from their front yard as Edward wrestled a pig easily two and a half times his size, and he was a large man having played college football as an offensive lineman. I was told shovels were used as weapons in an attempt to load Hamlette into the bed of the truck to no avail.

My friends told me when it became apparent that Edward was giving up for the day, they yelled across the street, "Are you going to try again tomorrow?"

He said, "Yeah, I have to. Why?" I'm sure his question of "why" was in hopes someone might help him.

They answered, "Ok, good! We're hoping to sell tickets!"

What Edward had to do to win was put plywood in the bed of his truck and make a wooden ramp into the bed. Hamlette didn't like the feeling or sound of her hooves on the metal. Once he placed the plywood in the truck, there were no problems. He said Hamlette went right in without hesitation. All those hours spent on Saturday fighting and losing to a pig were wasted, other than humor for neighbors and family stories, when all that was needed were a couple of sheets of plywood.

Technically, Hamlette was too big and too old to eat. Usually, pigs are butchered when they're much younger. I, more than anything, think we finally got rid of Hamlette due to her destructiveness and cost of feeding. I remember spending lots of time at a feed store in Ramsey, Indiana picking up food for all our animals, and for a little less than two years, Hamlette was the majority of it. She'd even eat the goat's food sometimes.

When my sister and I came home from our parents' houses that Sunday, the pig was nowhere to be found. After it was explained to my sister what happened, she cried declaring she'd never eat any of Hamlette. I don't know if she did or didn't. I did. Hamlette was tough due to her age, but every time I bit into anything I knew came from that pig, I smiled.

Flea Market Lucy:
The Bearded Lady's Daughter

Every time Lucy was arrested, she would say to herself, "This is the last time," and every time, she knew she was lying. She can't even remember all of them anymore. Lucy used to be able to, but now she can't. When she used to get arrested, one of the things she'd always do is recall each time prior. Now she remembers most, but she's quite sure it's not all.

The first time she was only fifteen. She was caught stealing from a department store. She was stealing makeup with a friend. They'd taken makeup a few times before that and got away with it. Neither of their parents forbade makeup wearing, but none of their parents could afford to buy makeup. Lucy's parents didn't even ask where or how she got the makeup. If it weren't for the yelling and door slamming, her parents wouldn't even really know she existed.

When they showed up at the police station to get her, they seemed so mad, which implied a level of concern for her. They were furious with her, but she quickly understood it was a front for the police. Oh, how they didn't realize what was happening. She was such a good girl. She'll be with a counselor as soon as possible. None of that was true. They stopped at Burger King on their way home from the police station. She even remembered they put tomato on her Whopper though she ordered without tomato. They always did that. "They always mess up 'to go' orders. They fuck you every time at the drive-thru," her dad would say.

Those were the days of growing up in Panama City, Florida, also known to folks living there as The Redneck Riviera. Her dad worked at a used car lot washing cars. His name was Rick. He'd been in and out of trouble his entire life, too. She was more like her dad than her mom. He was a small-time wannabe hustler. Any scam he could get in on in an attempt to make a few extra bucks by ripping off tourists from Tennessee and Kentucky, he was in.

His favorite was pretending to sell stolen gold chains to guys in their early twenties and late teens. They fell for it often. The deal is too good to let get away. Fifty bucks for a big gold chain would be a no-brainer, if only it were real. Since Rick got the chains for next to nothing, the markup on them was more than on real gold at a jewelry store where there might be five hundred dollars worth of gold in a chain and is sold for two thousand. Rick paid five or ten bucks for his fake chains. He'd sell loads of them during spring break, but he'd also raise the price then. Drunken guys were even easier targets than usual.

Rick later recruited Lucy into this scam. Once she was in her mid-teens, she could sell the chains easier than he could. The guys, attempting to impress her, would buy the chains at an even higher price and far more often. It seems like it was more about impressing the cute girl than missing a deal. Rick would give her half of each chain sold after the cost of the chain, but he sold more than twice as many with her helping. It was a good deal for him until they got caught and both arrested.

Lucy never wanted to help him. She felt coerced and helped him anyway. That was the second time she was arrested. Rick never even apologized. On the way home from the police station, they stopped at a Chinese buffet. Lucy loved all you can eat crab legs. She'd spend her time getting the meat out of the thin, rubbery legs and filling a bowl she'd filled halfway with butter. Then she'd eat it like crab leg butter porridge.

Lucy's mom is another story. Rick met Lucy years ago in the 70s when they both worked at a traveling carnival. Rick was the guy pressuring young men to play games to win junk teddy bears for their dates. He had "the gift of gab" as he called it. Some don't consider it a gift. Lucy's mom was in the so-called "freak show". She was the bearded lady. Her name was Annie.

Unlike many bearded ladies, Annie actually had a beard. She was picked up by the sideshow as a baby. The carnival found her in eastern Kentucky in the central Appalachian Mountains after hearing a rumor about a couple who had a bearded little girl. Her parents were uneducated and very poor. They sold her to the carnival for next to nothing. Annie grew up in the carnival. She never knew her parents, and the carnival manager didn't know them other than buying the baby. What's more unethical, buying a baby or selling one?

Annie was very self-conscious about her beard. By the time she was a teenager, she would often get in trouble for shaving it off. She got beat a few occasions and threatened often. She never really even knew how old she was. She presumed she was born in the mid to late fifties. In the mid-seventies, as the freak shows started coming under fire, the carnival manager reckoned she was twenty. It was at this time that the carnival rolled into central Florida, picking up Rick.

In the beginning, Annie was embarrassed about her beard and shied away from Rick. On one of the nights she shaved off her beard, she ran into Rick. They were in love ever since. Both had awful childhoods and could relate to each other through their torture and suffering.

After about a year of being in love and employed by the carnival together, they left the carnival with big dreams. They got married in Tennessee and drove to Florida where they began their life together. Two years later, Annie was pregnant.

Rick was born outside of Albuquerque, New Mexico. His parents were conspiracy theorists that thought the US government would eventually declare martial law like a terrible Hollywood movie. His father often beat him for no other reason than he was intoxicated. His mother would beat him the day after his father beat her.

He ran away when he was fifteen, stealing their car. He never spoke to either of them again. He knew nothing about his parents other than their names. He didn't know where they were from or even who his grandparents were. He didn't recall ever hearing his father speak of them. His mother only told awful stories of her parents leaving her with people she didn't know for long periods of time just to show up later to retrieve her. Many of the people she was left with took advantage of her. She often told Rick how good he had it compared to her life.

By the time Lucy was in school, Annie made money selling plastic junk in flea markets and swap meets. Sometimes it was knock-off toys for kids. By the mid-80s, she'd started selling bootleg VHS tapes. In the early 90s, she'd moved into pirated CDs. All the while, Rick was running his scams trying to get that big score which never came and washing cars in the used car lot. She later realized he did the car washing merely to be able to report something to the IRS. Most of the money Annie made in the swap meets was never reported.

Rick was shot and killed when Lucy was 23, during the mid-90s. It was never clear to her what happened. The police report implied it had something to do with stolen tools he was trying to sell to a truck driver. They found his body along the side of the road with his truck on Alligator Alley in southern Florida. He'd been missing for a few days, but that wasn't uncommon. After Rick's death, Lucy told her mother she wanted out of Florida.

She'd then been arrested many times, and things seemed to be going downhill quickly. She'd never finished high school and dropped out at sixteen years old.

Annie agreed, and they decided they'd follow flea markets up and down the East Coast and into the Midwest. They had a few suppliers of sorts for most of their products. They started selling knock-off Beanie Babies along with their VHS tapes, DVDs, and CDs. They could get them delivered or pick them up along the way.For a few years, this worked out pretty well.

They had enough money to buy a cheap but relatively reliable RV. They lived in it traveling all over the Midwest and East Coast. Things were going pretty well until Annie started getting sick. Annie wasn't a fan of hospitals or doctors. In the winter of 2000, in the small town of Somerset, Kentucky, she reluctantly asked Lucy to take her to the emergency room because she was having too much trouble breathing.

Annie died in that Kentucky hospital a few days later from lung cancer. She'd had it for years. The doctor at Lake Cumberland Hospital told her he didn't know how Annie lived as long as she did. That was of no comfort to her. All she could think was her mom had been suffering for who knows how long. Annie smoked all of Lucy's life. Lucy never smoked again after that day.

For the next few years, she found herself alone doing what she'd been doing most of her life, working flea markets and dealing in nickels and dimes not knowing where she'd find herself by the time she was forty. This worried her. She'd never even been in love. Due to her father, she didn't have much respect for men. They all seemed scheming to her, either scheming to make a couple of dollars or scheming to get in somebody's pants. For either of those endeavors, she had no respect.

At thirty-six years old, she was working a flea market in Shipshewana, in northern Indiana. It was fall, mid-October, and the market would be closing soon for the season. One afternoon, she was looking at some produce in a vegetable stands. A seemingly nice man started talking to her. He was the farmer of that stand selling his goods. That time of year, it was mostly pumpkins and gourds and so forth.

Lucy always thought she was attractive, but her background and history made her very self-conscious about herself. She didn't have a lot of self-esteem, and most men she'd met and been with weren't pleasant to either talk with or look at. This man, however, was both. He was polite and handsome, a tall, thin man wearing denim pants, nice shirt, cowboy boots and hat.

His name was Sam Dunn, and he often referred to himself as a "true Hoosier" being born and raised in Indiana. He'd farmed his entire life both on someone else's farm and now his own. He'd gone through a messy divorce, and for the last few years, he'd lived alone only having his hired hands on his farm. He mostly sold vegetables to local grocery stores and farmers' markets. He did the market occasionally himself because he liked the interaction with the different people he'd sometimes meet.

Lucy and Sam hit it off immediately. He was so inherently different than her dad and most men she'd ever met. Those last couple weeks of the auction and flea market, they had dinner together every night. When the auction wrapped and it was time for Lucy to move on, he didn't want her to go. It seemed sudden to both of them, but he asked her to stay with him on his farm.

For the next several months, she stayed with him. He had a lovely white, two-story, picturesque farmhouse with a complete wrap-around porch with a swing on each side just outside of town on the east side. Every morning, she'd wake up and fix him coffee and breakfast. He told her, every morning that she made the best biscuits and gravy he'd ever had. At night, she'd fix dinner. He told her he loved everything she cooked. She never once in her life was told she was a good cook. In fact, she couldn't recall ever being complimented on anything unless it was some grift. She'd never felt anything like how it made her feel, and to top it off; it quite scared her. She thought his kindness may be his scam.

Though the growing season was over, he still had a lot of work that needed doing. He had a small tree farm for Christmas trees. It was a u-cut farm, so not a whole lot was required. He did need to get the fields ready for the customers to hike around in while looking for the perfect tree.

That Christmas was the best Christmas Lucy ever had in her life. She and Sam spent those winter months warming themselves next to his woodstove telling each other about their lives and experiences. When spring arrived, Lucy began trying to contact her suppliers for things to sell at flea markets, Sam asked her not to. He didn't want her doing that anymore. He wanted her with him, working in his vegetable booth, side by side, so she did that very thing. It was the happiest time of her life. She worked his vegetable stand with him when he wasn't working the farm.

A few years later, a corporate farm offered to buy Sam's farm. Sam had contract farmed for years. Some companies would pay him for a specific amount of a particular crop. His farm had grown so much that he started leasing land from different people in the county. This was different from contract farming. This company wanted to purchase his farm. They were going to rotate corn and soybean on the majority of it. Some of it may eventually be used as a wind farm. He could keep his farmhouse and a few acres around it, but the rest would be gone.

Sam and Lucy never married, and as he mulled over this decision, she felt a bit slighted because he wasn't considering her feelings on the matter. He spoke to her about it, but he never asked her opinion or how she felt. One evening, as he was considering it, she wondered why he didn't care how she felt about it. His shock surprised her. He then told her he did consider her feelings, and that as far as he was concerned, they were married. He just didn't think she was interested in marriage since she never brought it up. He wasn't sure if she even wanted to stay. He confessed he thought she might leave him any night while he was asleep. He said every morning, when he woke up, he was always thankful that she was still there. They decided to keep the farm and not sell it. They also got married.

One Saturday afternoon, Lucy was in town walking down Harrison St. and spotted a house for sale. Homes in town on Harrison St. are used as businesses. Most of them are antique shops. She went to the door, and it was open. She walked in and thought to herself, "What if I owned a diner?" She spoke with the current owner and got some information. That night, she asked Sam what he thought about her opening a small diner there serving breakfast and lunch. Sam was immediately excited by Lucy's idea. The next day, they went back to the shop and spoke with the owner. Sam could afford the place outright, so no need to involve a bank.

That winter, Lucy worked with local contractors to transform the shop into a diner. Everything that could be bought used was bought from antique shops there in Shipshewana. A few things did need to be purchased new, but they did their best to make it a home of a diner. Lucy worked tirelessly testing different recipes and dishes. Sam and his farm hands tested and loved everything she cooked. They were the happiest group of guinea pigs east of the Mississippi.

By that spring, Lucy was ready. She hired a couple of waitresses and kitchen staff. The menu was planned, and she was prepared to serve the best short order foods in northern Indiana to the crowds coming in for the Shipshewana Auction and Flea Market. From then on, Lucy's diner was a regular spot for locals and people showing up to town for the auction. Hanging on the wall near the cash register looking out over the dining area was the only picture she and her mother together when Lucy was a child. Annie's beard, visible in the photo as she holds tiny Lucy in her arms, looks over the diner. Everyone loved their meals at the Bearded Lady's Daughter's Diner.

The Frog Gig

We had a good night, but we'll get to that. In the summer of 1990, I moved back to southern Indiana to live with my dad. I was previously living in Louisville, Kentucky with my mom, but I didn't care a lot for living in Louisville. I grew up in southern Indiana, and I preferred living in the country. I also got into a lot of trouble and was afraid of getting in more. I'd only lived in Louisville a year. Before that, I grew up in Indiana. My dad lived in the small town of Marengo in Crawford County in southern Indiana. I'd lived in neighboring Harrison County before.

I'd never lived with my dad before. We spent a lot of time together, but I'd never lived with him. He and his brother bought about twenty acres on Whiskey Run Road, or, at least that's what we were told the name of it was. When we moved in, the post office officially called it Route 2, but everyone in town called it Whiskey Run Road. In the late 90s, all the official routes were given road names for emergency crew issues. Our Whiskey Run Road was changed to Hogtown Road. Apparently, at some point in the past, there was a large pig farm somewhere on the road.

The three of us lived there, my dad, my uncle, and me. Since I'd not lived with my dad before and both of them were single, in a lot of ways, it was as if three guys were living together. I was only fifteen at the time.

We had a lot of good times there, too many to recall, but one night, in particular, my dad wasn't home. It was my uncle, his son Fredo (his name is Fred, but his family nickname was Fredo - he didn't live with us) and me at home that Saturday night. My dad wasn't there as he played music in bands back then. He was a guitar player. It was one of the nights his band had a gig. We'd all fished for years, but my uncle often talked about going frog gigging. When he was younger, he and his friends would go. My cousin and I'd never gone before, and we talked him into taking us.

Frog gigging is a way of hunting frogs. You have a long pole, often a cane pole, with a trident on end. One person holds a flashlight while the other or others try to spear the frogs. It's not as easy as it sounds, and it wasn't something I perfected as I only did it once. I think, in total, I gigged three frogs that night and missed a lot, intentionally.

There's a creek in the side yard of the house, but we never saw frogs there big enough to eat, just small ones. There was, however, a pond on our neighbor's property. The gentleman who owned it didn't live there, but he did take care of it. It was already nighttime, and he'd left for the evening. We didn't exactly get his permission to gig his pond. What I mean by that is we didn't ask at all. We just decided to go.

We packed up what we needed. Fredo is three years younger than I, so that puts him at 12. We had our gigs, flashlight, and bag for the caught frogs. Fredo and I were quite excited, as we'd heard so many stories about frog gigging over years. We were also excited because you can hear the frogs in that pond hundreds of yards away. We sprayed each other with bug spray as no one wanted any ticks. Ticks are quite an issue out in the woods and fields there. We all put on long pants, too, despite the heat, and we set out.

The house is on a gravel road, so that's where we started. We walked west until directly across a field from the pond. In order to stay out of sight in case the neighbor showed up as he would sometimes show up at night. We kept to the edge of the road and didn't use the flashlight. It was already completely dark. The sun was long asleep, and all we heard were crickets, frogs and our footsteps crunching the gravel. The lightning bugs left their small trails as we cut through the black summer heat.

Once we got into the field, we switched on the flashlight to see our way. Walking through fields can be risky business. Large rocks and briars can cause damage like twisted ankles, large cuts, and sprained wrists from falling having got your feet tangled in weeds and so forth. We didn't have any issues getting most of the way there until we got right to the pond. Right next to it is a barbed wire fence, the kind designed to keep animals and people in or out of something. In this case, it was most certainly designed to keep us out.

After working our way through the fence in the dark, we had to climb a small but very steep bank which is the dam that was built on the side of a sloping hill to hold the water running down the hill from rains to create the pond. This dam was steep, but not tall. I guess it's maybe six or eight feet tall. It's not a deep pond. It's what people call a "cow pond". Cow ponds are usually deep enough to cool the cows but so deep the water goes over their heads.

After we got to the top of the dam, my uncle then asked which one of us wanted to hold the light as he'd gig first to show us how to do it. I volunteered. He told me, "What you want to do is shine low. We want to see them from a bit of a distance. When that light hits their eyes, they kind of freeze a bit. That gives us time to walk a little towards them. When we get to 'em, you try to hit 'em right behind their eyes. That's the larger part. There's not much there to hit, so aim behind their eyes for the head and body."

As we began our way around the pond, it didn't take long to spot one. This frog was massive compared to any frog I'd seen during the day before. My uncle excitedly whispered, "Hang on! There's one right there! Y'all see it? It's right there!" We agreed we did, and he said, "C'mon, boys! I'll show you guys how to do this!" We cautiously sneaked closer and closer towards the frog while I steadily kept the light beaming on the eyes. The frog never even blinked.

Uncle Fred held up his hand signaling for us to stop walking. You don't throw the gig like a spear. You jab with it, never letting go of the gig. First shot, Uncle Fred got the frog. There it was, at the end of the gig, a rather large frog, dead. He said, "Now, not all of 'em will die like this. Some of them will still be alive." The thought of that bothered me, but I didn't say anything. He pulled the frog off the gig and slid it into the bag we tied to Fredo's waist as he volunteered to carry them.

The thought of not killing the frog immediately made me offer to keep shining the light saying, "I'll keep doing this! I like it! Let Fredo try first", so it was Fredo's turn. I kept the light at the low angle. Uncle Fred directed as we crept around the pond's edge. Then, there they were, the frog's eyes peeking up from the water's edge, just off the bank. We froze until Uncle Fred started going towards it. This time, he put Fredo in the front and me just behind holding the light. A few feet from the frog, Fredo slowly drew back the gig and jabbed! Once the splash was over, there was no frog. He'd missed.

Uncle Fred said, "Ok, that's okay. We'll get 'em next time!" After a few more words of direction about "behind the eyes," we took back off around the pond. A couple more attempts later, Fredo hit one. It wasn't a large frog, but Uncle Fred said it was big enough to cook. This frog didn't die. It was squirming in pain on the end of the cane pole with the 4-tined gig going through its body. This bothered me, and the thought of it still does to this day. Uncle Fred took the frog off, put it in the bag and said, "Alright, alright, alright! Good job, boys! Now it's Jerry's turn."

I'd dreaded that from the moment I saw that first frog on Uncle Fred's gig, but there was no way out at this point. I was fifteen and didn't want to look like a wimp. Things were a bit different in the late 80s and early 90s. Lots of pejorative words for guys who wouldn't do "guy" things back then. Fredo was my younger cousin, and I didn't want him to think I was grossed out by it. He looked up to me back then, so I had to do it.

With some coaching, Fredo was holding the light just right, and after a few yards, we spotted one. It was a huge one, the biggest one we'd seen all night.

I said, "Fred, that frog is gigantic. Why don't you do this one? If I miss, it'll get away." That was simply an attempt to get out of it.

He said, "Oh no! That's nothing. We'll get bigger ones. That's a nice one, but it's not as big as you think. They get much bigger than that."

As we began our approach, Uncle Fred put me in the front just as he did with Fredo. He was in the middle with Fredo right on the edge with the light. Fred was in my ear, "OK, so slowly, slowly. Right here. Now take your aim," so I drew back aiming for right behind the eyes. As I jabbed towards the frog, I recall closing my eyes. It didn't matter. I hit the frog. When I pulled it back, it was as I'd hoped. It was dead. That was a great relief to me, but the weight of the frog now dangling from the end of the gig bothered me a bit.

It was like this for quite a while. Fredo would go, and then I would. After a few turns, Uncle Fred would take a turn. We'd miss some and hit some. After we got the hang of it, I say we hit about fifty percent of the time. After a few times around the pond, we maybe had ten to fifteen frogs in the bag. Fredo even said, "This thing is getting a little heavy!" I couldn't bear the thought of those frogs hanging on me and up against me, so I said, "Oh no! You can't back out now!" laughing as if to seem like I was joking. They laughed too, but I don't remember it being mentioned again.

As we were going around and around the pond, we were so interested in what was going on, we stopped paying attention to everything else. Suddenly, we were reminded of the neighbor and our lack of permission as his dogs began barking and running towards us. We all froze, looking into the eyes of those dogs running towards us like the frogs we'd been catching with the light as they watched their doom coming straight at them. I broke the terrified, frozen silence with a loud yell of, "RUN!"

The neighbor's house was a few hundred feet away, and he had a few dogs. I don't remember exactly how many, but maybe three or four. After our broken hesitation, we were running. Nothing was going to catch us, except, of course, the barbed wire fence we'd forgotten about. We were wholly tangled in it. Fredo had the flashlight and got the frog bag tangled in the wire. I was caught in both pants and shirt. Uncle Fred was helping Fredo with the frogs. I kept working the fence and looking up to see the dogs.

I heard Uncle Fred say, "OK, you're out!" and Fredo, along with the flashlight, left the scene like a bullet, straight and fast. Fred and I were left, in the dark, tangled in barbed wire with what felt like impending doom heading our way as we could see the flashlight bouncing away and getting smaller.

We both finally got out and took off running. As we were running through the field in the dark, we could see the flashlight bouncing away through the darkness. Uncle Fred said, "He left us in the dark! I can't believe he left us!" I remember thinking the same, and now, looking back, I think it was probably his best plan.

As he said that, I was suddenly picking myself up from the ground. I fell into a deep hole. As I climbed out, it seemed like it was about chest deep. Fred stopped ahead and turned around to look for me. I stood up, looked towards the dogs. They were still coming and were about at the fence. Fred and I took off again. I caught up with him. He asked, "What happened?" I replied, "I fell in a hole!"

We were about two-thirds through the field, and I fell in another hole! This one hurt a bit, but fear had me. Fred didn't stop this time. As I stood up, I looked back. The dogs stopped chasing but were still aggressively barking, so I took back off.

Once I got to the gravel road, Uncle Fred was waiting for me. We stood there watching the dogs and very much out of breath. Once we caught our breath, we started walking back to the house.

It's not a long walk, and mostly we were laughing about the whole thing once the fear diminished. Frogs and dogs and fences and holes, it was all quite funny, and when we got back to the house, there was Fredo on the porch waiting for us. As we walked through the front yard, he said, "We lost some of the frogs! I don't know what happened!"

I said, "They probably fell out when we got tangled in the wire but maybe when you were running, leaving us in the field in the dark while you bolted with the flashlight."

We all laughed, and Fredo said, "Hey! After you both yelled 'run', I was out of there! I just happened to be the one with the light!"

Uncle Fred jokingly said, "Yeah, but you didn't have to leave us in the dark!"

The next morning, my dad was there. He got home late after we'd all gone to bed. We told him all about it. Everyone thought it was funny, and sure enough, we'd lost at least half of the frogs somewhere between the pond and the house, in tangled wire or bouncing through a field in the dark. My dad laughed at us and said, "That's what you all get for sneaking over there without permission! He's had them dogs since we've lived here! Didn't y'all even think of that before you left?" Nope, not a single one of us considered the dogs. We thought of everything except the risk. My dad said, "Buncha dummies," and laughed at us.

Blank Page

I saw her riding her bicycle towards the bar about a block away. I sat outside getting some fresh air as it was a fantastic night, fresh air almost reminiscent of early fall despite it still being high summer. I sat on a bench speaking with a friend as she waited to cross the street at the crosswalk, pushing a yellow and white classic beach cruiser style bike complete with a basket on the front.

I first met Page a few years earlier at work. When she first started working there, we did not work in the same department, but I saw her around the building often. She is beautiful, and I must admit that I tried to see her when I'd walk through the building.

When she transferred to my department, I was happily surprised. I recall the very first conversation I had with her. I walked into the discussion. I wasn't initially part of it. She was explaining how she doesn't like that Socrates's wife is, according to her, "highly mistreated in Plato's work." She even knew Socrates's wife's name "Xanthippe." She also knew the meaning of the name "blonde/yellow horse." I instantly knew that Page was, most likely, the smartest person I'd met so far at work.

As I sat outside on the bench, Page approached me wearing a grey sundress with spaghetti straps. It was warm enough for that top, but as the sun set, I knew it was going to be chilly. She has almost jet black, very curly hair, but she had it up off her neck. This, of course, accentuated her elegant necklines connecting her shoulders and chin. She has near alabaster skin save a few freckles. Her eyes are brown with green flakes.

When first meeting Page, the most obvious thing about her is how pretty she is. The second thing noticed is her high-pitched, cartoon-like voice. I've told her time and time again that she needs to try to get work doing voice-overs for cartoons. She can't do voices, but her voice is voice enough for a cartoon, like Yeardley Smith from The Simpsons. Smith does one voice save a few roles here and there. She's made a career doing the voice of Lisa Simpson.

As I stepped out of the restaurant to the sidewalk, she said, "Hi, Jerry! How are you?"

"Hey, Page! How are you? You look great, as always!" I said.

"No, I don't. I'm getting fat," she said, lightly patting her tiny belly.

I chuckled and said, "Just take the compliment! You always look great!" After a few more pleasantries and a hug, I suggested we go inside and have a drink.

She ordered a cider, and we began to go into a great conversation. The situation with Page is this. I've known her for years, and we have a lot in common. We read the same books. We like the same music. We watch the same movies. We admire the same people's work. Despite all these commonalities, when I asked her out, she turned me down, saying, "I don't date people I work with." There was more to it than that which I did not know, but the worst part of her rejection was her very next boyfriend turned out to be a guy we worked with. That hurt a bit, but I'm a grownup and can handle rejection.

Page and I remained friends over the years. In fact, we became rather good friends based on the commonalities and very similar senses of humour, dark, inappropriate and twisted senses of humour, the type of humour that often repulses people. In our minds, nothing is too soon, and nothing is off limits.

The background we have together is a bit intimate. We tend to be a bit more telling in what we share with each other than I usually do even with other close friends. I don't know why.

Perhaps it's because, despite rejecting me, I've always still been a bit smitten with her. Not that I pine over her. I acknowledge that I hold romantic feelings for her. I never tried to lie to myself and assume she didn't know. I know she knows, and I've thought she sometimes regretted turning me down which is, most likely, a vanity and wishful thinking.

As we sat at the bar inside the restaurant drinking and catching up, I remembered that I'd been a bit worried about her. Some of the text messages she'd sent recently were a bit out of character. The messages leaned a bit to the sad. This is why I invited her out that night. I wanted to check on her so to speak. I invite her out a lot. She rarely shows up. Her boyfriend didn't like me, not at all. He knows I asked her out, and he knows she likes me. He's not fond of me, and it makes him like me less knowing she likes me. Ugly people love to wear ugly things like envy and pity.

I didn't dwell on my thoughts much. I prefer active listening. There are very few things more distasteful than passive listening. We were wrapped up in a conversation about Page's disliking of chickens. She doesn't like chickens. I can't think of anything cuter than a dislike of chickens.

"I fucking hate chickens! They're so fucking stupid! I mean, I'd never hurt a chicken, but I do like pissing them off. When I see chickens in a pen, I'll throw stuff in to make them think I've thrown food. Then I'll run around to the other side of their pen and throw in more leaves or whatever, so they run to the other side thinking it's food again! God! I love pissing off chickens! They're like battered wives, too! There's only one cock with a group of chickens, and he treats them like shit! They just let him, too, but you know, since there are so many chickens, his shittiness probably doesn't feel so bad. It's spread out evenly among the chickens, so it's not that big of a deal. Then again, who gives a shit about the emotional state of a chicken? Fuck chickens! I don't care if they even have emotional states, and if they do, who gives a shit!? It's a fucking chicken! Fuck chickens!"

We laughed as this went on for a good twenty minutes. Her laughter breaths bubbly new air into me like the giddiness exploding from a child's smile while eating Pop Rocks for the first time. I, of course, egged on her giddiness. She was laughing and drinking her cider. I couldn't drink. For the last three weeks, I'd been asked by my doctor not to drink. I'd been having some minor issues with my gallbladder, and the doctor asked me just to avoid alcohol for a bit. Fine, I'm not much of a drinker anyway.

The time at the bar went on for a couple of hours and a couple more ciders for her and Arnold Palmers for me. We laughed and talked and just went back to being friends without skipping a beat. We'd not seen each other in seven months or so. We did speak quite a bit via messaging, email and so forth, always making vague plans that fell through. They seemed half-hearted as we made them. We sent messages saying how much we missed each other.

I realized the bar was empty except for myself and Page. I suggested we get out of their way. I paid the tab, and we started out the door. It was dark. It was rather late. She was a bit tipsy. I didn't know exactly where she lived as she'd moved relatively recently, but there was no way I could let her walk her bike home alone. I told her I wasn't comfortable with her walking back alone. She didn't argue other than to say it was a long walk.

I said, "Long walk or not, I can't let you go alone. That's not polite. I wouldn't feel right. Besides, it wouldn't be very Jimmy Stewart-like of me to let you walk home alone." She roared with laughter and asked what Jimmy Stewart had to do with it.

I said, "Hey, Jimmy Stewart was a great man, or, at least, a culmination of the characters he played in movies was a great man. All I'm saying is one could do much worse than Jimmy Stewart when looking for a role model. I'd like to think when I die, someone says, 'Jimmy Stewart would approve of Jerry's life.' I'd be good with that." Page's laughter grew, and we began our long walk to her place.

As we walked down the very busy Bardstown Road in the Highlands, a trendy neighborhood for twenty and thirty-somethings in Louisville, KY, passing all the bars and restaurants that were still open. Page pushed her beach cruiser with the basket on the front in her sundress talking away with her hypnotic voice. I accidentally stepped outside the scene and looked at us as if I were one of the people sitting at the tables in front of the bars watching us walk by. There was me with my blondish red hair with my messenger bag cross-body style, black button-down shirt and khaki cargo shorts with boat shoes and sporting brightly-colored, non-matching. barely visible socks peeking up out of my shoes. I am 13 years older than Page. As I saw this, I felt like I was in a Woody Allen story.

This amused me as I am a fan of Woody Allen's movies. The particular movie brought to my mind was "The Mighty Aphrodite". Not that Page is a prostitute, but Page and the Mira Sorvino character have two similar traits: the voice and the fact that they both talk a lot. That's not a bad thing. I enjoy listening to Page talk. I listen and ask questions. She speaks moving from one topic to the next without regard for segue and disregarding if the previous issue was even brought to a close.

About forty-five minutes into our walk, I had to stand guard outside some bushes beside a convenience store as she peed. When she stepped out of the bushes, from her angle, I was lit from behind by street lights.

She said, "You seem very lonely standing there!" That was all there was to that because at that moment, she spotted a bar she likes to frequent. "OH! Let's have a drink! You can sit with me while I get shit-faced, and since you're walking me home, there are no worries about me getting drunk!" She laughed and dashed happily across the street with her bike towards the bar.

As we entered, I realized she was well-known by the staff there. The bouncer, bartenders and quite a few regulars knew her all saying "hello" and a few other niceties. I got her a drink, and we then sat outside on the patio. It was here that the "Woody Allenness" atmosphere of the story increased a bit.

Page now began repeating a few things: "I think what people do when they're drunk is what they want to do but are too afraid to do normally," "What people say when they're drunk is what's really on their minds," and, curiously, "You have shitty timing, Jerry." This last one, I didn't understand until a little later in the evening. She just said it while there twice without reference to what she meant. She said all these things quite a few times.

She got quiet for a moment, looked at me and said, "I don't know why my boyfriend keeps me around."

This saddened me. Page didn't realize her boyfriend is the lucky one in the relationship. I know too many people that don't understand this. I looked at Page and said, "Why don't you realize you're better than him?"

She was quiet for a moment again, and then she said, "I know he loves me. He loves me more than he's loved anyone else before me, but I don't love him that much. I certainly don't love him as much as he wishes I would love him. Maybe I don't even love him."

'Maybe I don't even love him.' I don't know why this sentence stuck with me the way it did. I've thought about it a lot. Don't we know if we love someone, and "love" only exists as a two-way street? It cannot be a one-way street. That's not love. That's admiration and adoration. Love requires mutual feelings on both sides.

"I think… I think we can have more than one soul mate. I mean, I don't believe in any kinda Jesus or God bullshit. I mean someone that fits us, someone that suits us. Does that make sense?" she asked me as she drank some more.

"Of course, especially if we consider how long we live nowadays compared to when the concept of 'soulmate' was invented. I'm not sure, but it probably came about back when our lifespans were like thirty or some dumb shit like that," I half-jokingly said.

"Yeah, of course, but I think even more so than that," and she stopped, taking a drink.

In my thoughts, she was talking about polyamorous love, or, what an old friend and I termed, "a polyphony of love." My friend had a relationship with a married woman that tore him down from the inside out. He was one of the most joyful, fun-loving people I knew. When his relationship with her deepened, I began seeing the darkening shades of despair on him. Despair is the sickness unto death. I caught up with him one day as I drove down a busy street. He was riding his bike in the rain. When I pulled up next to him, I could see that he was crying. Rain doesn't hide our tears like we think it does.

I didn't press that conversation with Page. In fact, we only sat there long enough for her to have one drink, but we stayed there for maybe an hour talking as she drank slowly. Then we left. She said her goodbyes to all those she knew in the bar. Our conversations in the bar were mostly about her failing relationship. We did talk about other things, not all sad. We were laughing in the bar a bit. The night had taken a turn by this point. It most certainly began turning from external topics like her dislike of chickens to "she and I."

Walking out of the parking lot back to the sidewalk of the still very busy Bardstown Road, she brought up something that she would later bring up again. She asked me if I was ever mad at her for turning me down with the reason of not dating co-workers then her next (and current at the time) boyfriend being a co-worker. All I said was, "It's a bummer, but I'm not a bitter person, Page. That's not my style."

She said, "Of course it's not. You've far better taste than that. You're like Oscar Wilde!"

It was here that she went into a lengthy discussion about why exactly she said "no" to going out with me. In fact, I'd only just met her then. We'd known each other maybe a month or two. What I didn't know was that at that time, she was being stalked by an ex who was a co-worker. He'd made her days terrible following her around at work, after work and everywhere she went. She recanted a nasty breakup. Then she stopped talking and walking, turned and looked at me and said, "You've got really shitting timing. You know that, Jerry? Really shitty timing." Then she went back to walking. The conversation changed abruptly.

"He broke up with me the other day. No one knows that, Jerry.", She said. I didn't know what to say. "We got back together the next day, but he dumped me." she continued. She told me about how horrible she'd felt. All that went through my mind was throughout the night, all she'd done is badmouth him and rightly so. He's a dick. He comes from an upper-middle-class family. Both of his parents come from lower class families having worked their lives to achieve their level of success. This, of course, has skewed his views of reality. I didn't know him well. He's never liked me for many reasons beyond the obvious. He's envious of me over another girl from earlier, and he's envious of me because of my position at work amongst other things. I had a job he thought he's entitled to. This sense of entitlement is why most people I knew thought he was a prick. He was born on second base and thought he hit a double.

Me? I thought he was a prick because he has no sense of empathy. He's a typical conservative, Ayn Randian, self-made, bootstrapping, "island unto himself" kind of guy who says ridiculous things like, "those homeless people just need to get jobs" and other nonsensical things and rejects simple facts like we're not all born into a world where our parents pay our way through college, don't abuse us, aren't raised in environments where criminal elements aren't considered "bad" and are never given encouragement at any point in our lives from any parental or authority figure. To such descriptions of life, he'd respond, "They need just to try harder." Why try harder for a system that pushes even harder against us if we try to better ourselves? Such people always view what they deem "successful people" as self-made people who they assume to have never, not once, had any help achieving anything in their lives. This, of course, is nothing more than bullshit. No one is an island unto herself. Such people are willing to take credit as if they are.

I said to Page, "Sometimes, Page, some people fall into things because of the ease of it. After a while, it's easy to confuse contentment with complacency."

She said, "Jerry, I don't think you'd fuck me if you had the chance." It was an odd and abrupt turn in the conversation.

"Quite the contrary, Page. I like to think I'm not a pig of a man, but I am a man nonetheless," I responded half-jesting.

She said, "I mean right now with me being drunk. You wouldn't fuck me like this even if I were begging you to."

As I was about to answer, she said, "What would Jimmy Stewart think about that?", and she then laughed.

Laughing, I replied, "Correct. You are correct. I couldn't fuck you in this situation. It would be difficult to say no. I strangely like the idea of you begging for it which bothers me, but I couldn't do it. Jimmy Stewart wouldn't approve of such." I laughed.

She stopped and looked at me again and said, "You have shitty timing, Jerry, really shitty timing."

We reached her apartment which is an old three-story house that'd been turned into apartments in the Highlands. It's a beautiful old house that would be marvelous to live in if I lived in it, not as a renter. I carried her bike up the few steps in the back door, and said, "OK, cool, Page. It's late and still a long walk, so I'm going to start heading back."

She said, "NO! I'm going to walk with you! It's a long walk. It's late, and I don't want you to be lonely. I'll go with you, and then you can drive me home from there."

I said, "Are you sure? That'd be great! It is an amazing night," and we began the long walk back to my car.

Instead of walking back down heavily lit and busy Bardstown Road, I asked if we could stay on Cherokee Road.

Cherokee Road is a residential street lined with giant trees whose limbs stretch out over the sidewalk and street with, hidden in the limbs and leaves, streetlights that leave beautiful spots of light shining through. These are old, full trees. These are big beautiful old houses. These are brilliant tall-grassed or ivy-covered yards. When we'd step out into the moonlight, I'd watch the light fall on her face and neck and hair.

This section of the night, at least for the first eighty percent of it, was filled with less intimate conversations. We spoke about books, her love of the band The Clash, movies (specifically Jimmy Stewart), our acceptance of an artist or poet having a muse but our dislike of someone ever referring to her or himself as a muse and many other things.

I told her that the night reminded me of a Woody Allen movie. She also likes Woody Allen movies and agreed. Her only disagreement was I'm not too old for her as Woody Allen is compared to his female co-stars in his more recent movies. She said it was a very romantic and intimate night. I agreed.

One conversation that stood out was about passion. Page was a bit focused on passion in relationships. It started as a conversation about how people we've known from our pasts who've ended up in abusive relationships which led us to discuss the movie "A Streetcar Named Desire" starring Marlon Brando. The character Stanley Kowalski was abusive, but that relationship certainly had a lot of passion. Page talked about how much she loved that movie. I said, "Well, Marlon Brando was a living Greek statue… a beautiful man." She agreed.

This led me to bring up a topic I think about a lot. Often, sex with people we don't like and even hate can be great because sex is as close to violence as we can get without going to jail. In fact, it can be a very violent act. This led us to discuss how some people can get lost in terrible relationships because the passion and sex can be fantastic despite the tragedy of the rest of the relationship.

I said, "Sex is certainly a form of escapism, too. Imagine very tragic conditions full of misery and even starvation. Sex can be a temporary relief when one doesn't have to consider the conditions of the rest of her or his life. At that moment, it's the pleasure of the sex."

I then asked her about the spelling of her name. The few women I've known named Page spelled it Paige. She said her mom preferred the spelling Page because it's like a blank sheet of paper in a book ready to be filled with words and thoughts. At that moment, I thought of Descartes, and I could not think of a better name in the world than "Page."

I asked about her childhood. She told me so much. She grew up very poor most of her life. She lived in welfare housing by age eight. Before that, she lived with her grandparents which she thinks of as the happiest time of her life. She told me stories of growing up, different people she'd known, events that have taken place and anything and everything that popped into my mind to ask, she answered.

She told me that she's never lived in any place that she was proud to call "home" other than her time as a child living with her grandparents. She loved living in the Highlands despite all the hippie, yuppie and yippie bullshit. She said the Highlands even deflects bullshit with its beauty.

I said, "It deflects all that bullshit by being full of more and different bullshit."

She laughed and said, "You're probably right!" We both agreed that there are few neighborhoods in the city that would allow people to walk around this late without fear of being harassed or robbed or worse.

A few blocks from the car, she began talking about her grandfather's death. His death was very difficult for her. I remember well when this happened. It was a grueling ordeal. He had a rough time. It's not a proper thing for me to recount this story as it is hers to give if and when she ever decides to. She started crying. I tried to comfort her, but I don't think I was very successful, and this made me feel a bit uneasy.

We got in my car, and I began dreading the night coming to a close. She almost fell into the passenger seat laughing and said, "If you're dating a woman that wants kids, make sure you drive this car! It is not child-friendly!" and she laughed. It's a small sports car. As we pulled away, I instantly began thinking of the longest route to take to get her back to her place. Despite it being a long walk, at most, it was going to be a ten-minute drive. As I rounded the curve on Willow Avenue towards Cherokee Parkway, she said, "Hey! Let's ride through the park! I've never been to the park at night! Let's go! It'll be great!"

At that moment, I couldn't think of anything better to have come out of her mouth. I feared the end of the night twice now, and both times, she'd suggested it continue. We'd drive through Cherokee Park, maybe park or walk around a bit. Who knew? What I did know is that the night wasn't ending yet.

Cherokee Park was designed by the same guy who created Central Park in Manhattan. It's beautiful and having only been to Central Park twice at that point, I could feel a resemblance of atmosphere, but Central Park is much grander, older feeling and as a non-New Yorker, less inviting. I'm sure it doesn't feel that way to New Yorkers. Cherokee Park is full of winding curves, dark woods paths, small open areas likes Central Park with small parking lots. As we drove around talking and talking, we'd spot the isolated cars that certainly had people making out or having sex in them.

We parked and got out near a fountain. We walked around a bit. I noticed the moonlight falling on the lines of her neck and ringlets of her hair. She was more beautiful at that moment than I'd ever noticed before. Her voice was more mesmerizing. Her eyes sparkled the silver reflected light of the moon. The glimmering stars spangled her pale skin. It was a perfect night. Not even Zeus, the god of rain, dared intervene on this night. Nothing could have made this night better.

In the darkness of Cherokee Park, we talked of darkness and which type darkness is the scariest. I told her of the darkness at my dad's house. He lives in the woods, and it's so dark in the forest that I sometimes seem to feel it penetrating my skin. She said the darkness at the edge of a campfire is the scariest darkness. I said, "Standing at the edge of darkness by a campfire may be the darkest darkness. The sounds of the forest are the scariest when standing at the edge of the darkness made by a campfire."

Our time in the park lasted hours. We walked. We parked. We drove. I couldn't stop looking at her in the car with the sunroof open and moonlight pouring in. The glow of the dashboard lights and wind in her hair seemed like some fantastic dream that I was desperately trying not to wake from.

I blurted out, "Page, this is the most romantic night in my life."

She turned her head to me and said, "I agree. This is the best night of my life. I don't want it to end. Let's drive all night until the sun comes up. Then we'll go have coffee and start all over!" Nothing in my life had ever made more sense than that did at that moment.

We drove in and out of Cherokee Park exhausting every single road we could find. Eventually, we drove until we found ourselves in Prospect, KY which is miles and miles away. We drove down River Road from Prospect all the way to downtown Louisville. I showed her one of my favorite places. It's the front of a building that has no structure attached to it. It's a facade. It seems to be on a pedestal as some monument, but I've never noticed a plaque indicating what it's for, and it is either old or made to look old. I can't tell. For many years, I've wanted to take pictures of it, and for many years, I'd forgot. Page said, "It's so odd and grandiose. I can't believe I've never seen it. You do need to take pictures of it. I don't think I've seen photos of it."

By this time, it was three thirty in the morning. We were closing in on the dawn, just a couple hours away, and we'd be having coffee. I, myself, had never even tasted coffee, but I was going to drink some coffee with her that morning, and then her phone rang. It was her boyfriend. They spoke briefly. The conversation seemed to end abruptly. Her tone changed at that moment. The proclaimed greatest night of our lives had suddenly come to an end. Without even asking, I began driving back towards her place. She was less talkative, and I had fewer questions.

When we got back to her place, she had me drive around to the back. I stopped the car. She took off her seatbelt. We hugged, and she got out of the car and said, "Bye, Jerry." I watched her walk into her house. Once she shut the door, I backed out of her driveway and drove home with the windows down, wind in my face and hair, and Zeus finally showed up with a very light drizzle stinging my arm and a little on my face.

I'd live my life over again and again, every broken heart, every moment of joy, every sad goodbye, every stretch of depression and every moment of boredom only to live this night

again, and I've still, to this day, never tasted coffee.

Fawn: 13.1.13

She knows her name is Fawn, or better yet, she knows that is her nickname. She is unit 13.1.13. She is an infiltration unit programmed to collect data. She understands she is a she. Fawn's programming allows her to manipulate her body as any deer would and far beyond it. She was programmed to infiltrate and collect data about all she can on the lives of deer in the Midwest region of the United States. She was missioned in the wild, and there she will remain until her battery drains. She will not grow. She will always appear to be a young female deer, and once her battery is nearing the end, she will self-destruct.

Her mechanical body is stronger than the other deer or any animal for that matter. Her chassis is manufactured from a titanium alloy-like compound. She is bulletproof to keep the danger from hunters at a minimum. Though it is most likely unnecessary since Fawn will know the hunters are there through her massive network of data collecting senses long before any of them ever even see her.

Fawn has ears, eyes, a nose and a mouth. Her exterior is sensitive to the touch, but those things, even though hers are much more developed than any living animal on earth, are nothing compared to her data collecting senses we don't see. Under her armor, she has sensors of all kinds. The eyes on her head see next to nothing compared to the X-ray and infrared sensors that point in all directions from her body. She hears into the ultra and infrasound ranges beyond any sonar systems known. This sonar system is not located in her "ears." The ears are just part of the disguise.

Fawn's nose is a data collecting system for smell, but it's not her only one. Fawn has scent sensing systems across her body that analyze and determine smells with more precision than any bear, better than mice whose nostrils work in stereo and independent of each other. If mice have stereophonic nostrils, Fawn's could be called quadraphonic. Because of her sense of smell, her tongue is used to house other essential functions. Sure, she pretends to eat and drink and make noises, but her tongue contains a mechanism that collects necessary elements that, when needed, creates an ointment of sorts that when applied to her synthetic skin and fur, becomes a rapid healing agent. Yes, her synthetic coat and skin have memory healing qualities to them, but with the aide of the ointment, she heals much faster when needed, and Fawn knows when it is required.

Her fur and skin are synthetic. Each strand of fur more sensitive than the fur of animals. Fawn knows if a butterfly flaps its wings over her back. Fawn can perceive the vast majority of things within a hundred meters of herself and even through most materials. She may not be able to see through steels, but her sonar gives her a topographical view of any metal object.

Fawn also has very advanced camouflage if necessary. In fact, her synthetic skin is heated to impersonate the heat of a warm-blooded animal. She's fixed with enough systems that human technology could only sense her as a deer. Our sonars, x-rays and infrared would surrender data of a deer. It's as if she's wearing a mask entirely through her body.

It was easy for her to infiltrate any deer herd. They're not particularly smart animals, and compared to Fawn, neither are humans. Deer are cautious and easily frightened which is how they've evolved and thrived. Fawn knows and understands this. She's watched many deer from afar before she ever tried to interact with them. She learned their ways and how to imitate them precisely. After a while of data collecting and analysis, she made her way into a herd rather easily. She's been with the same herd for years now though not a single deer that was in the herd when she joined it is still alive, not even the offspring of those are with her anymore. The grandchildren of those original deer are who she is with now.

Collecting data on deer is not her only priority. In fact, being a deer is just her disguise. She is also collecting data on all animals and plants in which she comes in contact. She has a lot of information on humans. She's noted they're not observant when operating vehicles on roadways. She's witnessed several deer killed by them.

Fawn gathered enormous amounts of data on squirrels and other rodents. She's collected information on trees and other plants in the area in which she lives. She's mapped her region precisely. The group she has been with has managed many square kilometers in the three generations she's been with them. She understands that soon she will need to move to a neighboring location to map that locale and to see if there are any vegetation and animal changes. In other words, she'll have to join a new herd.

Leaving and joining another herd is not an issue. It'll take some time to gather the new herd's trust, but with her exceptional skills of imitation, it won't take long at all. It's not like she's trying to trick primates, but that, too, isn't that difficult. Appearing as a young fawn, she poses no immediate threat to a herd of deer. For all they can reckon, she's merely a lost fawn who never seems to grow up, and they treat her as such.

Her x-ray and sonar systems have not only mapped the area, she's also mapped the underground cave systems and waterways. This made a particular note in her daily uplinks. She is connected to a central unit through a wireless network. She sends a daily log of all her collected data. Essential and vital information is returned to her. Her priorities change as needed.

Fawn's programming is updated, too, but with her massive processing units, her ability to learn and evaluate is beyond any computer known to humans. She is more significant than any machine humans have ever built. Fawn is a hybrid. She has many CPUs, half of them are digital, which is the most common, but the other half are highly advanced analog processors. In this sense, she has a neural system very similar to the human neural network, only it's far more sophisticated and still just as biological. Fawn is aware of everything she does. She is not merely a robot doing work.

Why does Fawn do this? It is her prime directive, her job. Yes, she could decide to do something else, but what would come of it? She's from somewhere else, somewhere far. She's a being that merely wishes to study this world and all its wonder without being suspected.

There are many others like Fawn. No, they're not all deer. Some swim deep in the oceans. Some live high in the mountains. Some fly the skies. Some walk amongst humans as humans. Within a few more generations, the entire globe will be mapped both above and below the surface and deep within the crust of the earth. The aquatic versions will have mapped the deepest regions of the ocean beyond the depths humans have plunged. They are also already far more knowledgeable of every planet and planetoid in our Sun's system. These infiltrators are already on all of them. When these infiltrators encounter each other, they make note and move on.

They're not only on this world and in our solar system. They're throughout the Milky Way on other planets. What do they want? What is their primary goal? In fact, what is signified with the word "their" regarding this? "They" seek out inhabitable planets and other intelligent life out of sheer curiosity.

This, dear readers, is a thought train written by a human. If I can dream up such beings with such technology, then what technologies exist that I can't even fathom at this point? Human understanding of science and technology is only in the most adolescent stage.

We can think of Fawn's camouflage and say, "that's absurd," but that is what people said about molecules. We couldn't see them. At that point, it was absurd to think something we can't see exists. We now know they exist. Fawn could be built of elements we don't know exist, elements not on our periodic table as there are holes in our periodic table.

Fawn can walk upright and carry things and speak in our language if she so pleased. Fawn could have tiny digits embedded in her "hooves" that allow her to manipulate tools when needed. Fawn could be carrying weapons we haven't imagined yet. It's not that Fawn is undetectable. It's that we do not, now, have the technology to detect her.

The point is this. If a group of beings, or even one being, is advanced enough to travel such great distances to get here, then what makes us think we would/could, at this stage in our scientific and technological adolescence, detect it or them? What makes us feel they couldn't study us without kidnapping and probing us? We could be examined from a perspective that is not perceivable to us, and we could be investigated thoroughly from this perspective. We need to dissect beings to study them if we want to know their internal workings. That doesn't mean we will need to do so in the future. Sensing mechanisms from an advanced culture may not need even to be close to us. Their technologies may, in fact, be able to penetrate us to our memories from childhood with an ability to download all our memories, even ones we struggle to remember. They could know our fears and our weaknesses with an ability to exploit these to a degree we can't even imagine at this point.

If Fawn is merely a robot to you, then you're missing the point of evolution. The only divinity we know is the ability to create. If we can create, then nothing is stopping us from recreating ourselves. What's preventing us from rebuilding the shaky foundation of our body by reorganizing, picking and choosing and restructuring our very DNA? We can intelligently redesign these bodies.

As of now, there is nothing intelligently designed about our fragile bodies. At any minute, our appendix can rupture and kill us. We can choke to death on our food because our breathing and eating apparatus are the same, which isn't the case with some animals (whales). We're incredibly susceptible to disease, and our bodies are frail when compared to other animals. Someday, we will have it within our power to change all these things and make ourselves into something different. Perhaps it will come to it one day that what we know as "us" will become "them" and will no longer be recognizable as "us" to the beings that will then be calling themselves "human" just as "we" would look at the original humanoid carrying human DNA would appear to us. We would not recognize each other as "we." Future beings calling themselves "human" will not look at us as "we." "We" will have become "them" to those humans.

Fishing and Soda and Pop

I cannot recall the first time I went fishing. I've gone fishing my entire life as far as I can recall. I remember going fishing as a small child and not enjoying it. What I did enjoy was throwing rocks into the pond, lake or river. I tried to enjoy it, but the way I was raised fishing is, to most and especially to kids, dull. We put bait on a hook with a float, cast it, and wait for a fish to bite. The wait can be maddening to a small child and some adults.

By the time I was nine or ten, the waiting didn't bother me as much. It still couldn't hold my attention for long, but it held it longer. By the time I was a teenager, it didn't bother me at all. In my twenties, I began enjoying the wait.

Most of my life we fished from the bank. We didn't have a boat. Around the time I turned eighteen, my pop bought a small fishing boat. From that point forward, we fished almost exclusively from the boat. Here's an interesting fact I learned making this transition from bank to boat fishing. When fishing from the bank, you often try your damnedest to cast to the center of the lake. When you're fishing from a boat, you spend most your time fishing as close to the shore as possible. That's not always true, of course, but it is a great deal of the time.

I grew up fishing for sunfish. Sunfish, also called panfish due to their shape, are often small and quite tasty which is why we fish for them. We call almost all of them bluegill, but in fact, we often catch as many redear, which also called shellcracker. They get their name because they've adapted to eating snails. We also catch crappie when we can. They're not as easy to catch, and they swim in large schools. When you do catch crappie, you typically catch a lot of them. They're quite a bit larger than bluegill and redear, but bluegill and redear are the ones we catch the most.

We also catch Pumpkinseed. They tend to be smaller. I've always assumed that's where they got their name. We occasionally do fish for catfish and bass, and sometimes we catch them while fishing for bluegill. Predominantly, we fish for panfish. The occasional catfish and bass are happy surprises.

We always eat what we catch as we're not sport or trophy fishermen. I grew up fishing primarily with my pop. I call my dad "pop". Typically when he'd take me fishing, his brother and kids would come, too. His kids are my double cousins. Since double cousins share both sets of grandparents, they've as many genetic similarities as half-siblings, and I have two of them. I grew up spending a lot of time with both of them as they're on both sides of my family.

Pop also has a younger brother who often went with us. He is eighteen years younger than my dad. He's only three years older than me, so he and I also spent a lot of time growing up together. We were more like cousins than uncle and nephew. In fact, when he started driving and I was hanging out with him and his friends, we agreed to say we were cousins instead of uncle and nephew in an always-failed attempt to make me appear older. I was somewhat short until a very late growth spurt at twenty-one years old. Calling me his nephew made me appear even younger than I actually was.

My parents are divorced. I lived with my mom and step-dad until I was fourteen. Moving in with my dad was kind of odd at first. The most extended amount of time he and I ever spent together were vacations, and that only lasted a week or so. We went to the same place every year, Herrington Lake in Danville, Kentucky. We stayed in rental cabins with almost the entire family on my dad's side. He and I were usually the ones who stayed the longest. We'd often get there on a Saturday and remain until the following Friday and sometimes Saturday. It was my grandpa's favorite place to go. When he passed away in the late 80s, our trips to Gwinn Island, the marina and resort we stayed at, became less and less frequent. It's now been years since any of us went.

There were many places we fished other than Herrington Lake closer to home. We often fished a pond everyone referred to as "Uncle Ed's Bluegill Factory." Ed was not our uncle. In fact, he was not related to us. He was my pop's friend's uncle. He was a nice guy who let us fish in his pond that was full of bluegill. One particular trip to Uncle Ed's, I was trying to catch bass as I'd gotten a little older. I walked to the side of the pond I'd never fished and never seen anyone else fish before.

There was a small fence that ran into the pond. Cows used this pond a lot, so that was to keep them on one side of it. I was casting along the fence and landed a fish. I was fishing for bass, so I assumed that's what I landed. The fish fought like a bass, too. When I pulled the fish from the water, it was a crappie. We didn't even know there were crappie in the pond. We spent the next hour or two reeling in nice crappie one after another. That was one of our best fishing days ever.

Another pond we went to occasionally was my uncle D's uncle's pond. Uncle D was my uncle by marriage. He'd married my dad's sister. I don't ever recall meeting uncle D's uncle while there. I also don't ever remember catching a lot of fish there either. My favorite thing about uncle D's uncle's pond is that we had to drive the cars through fields and down wide paths to get to it as it was deep inside the property. I mostly recall throwing rocks into rather than pulling fish out of this pond.

My dad's family is from Portland. Portland was originally a small town along the Ohio River west of the city of Louisville. As Louisville grew, it consumed Portland, and Portland became a neighborhood on the west side of Louisville. In fact, some call Portland "The West End". Living next to the Ohio River meant we fished in the Ohio River. I only recall two trips to the McAlpin Locks and Dam being good fishing days. Two weekends in a row, Pop, my uncle, his kids and I caught a ton of perch. We don't eat perch, but my uncle did use perch as fertilizer for his garden. I think both times we caught around sixty fish. My uncle had a nice garden in Portland.

I grew up in Indiana until I was 14. Then my mom and I moved to Louisville. The year before that, my dad bought property in Indiana and moved there. I, having spent almost all my life in Indiana, did not like living in Louisville, and moved to my dad's house in less than a year. It is there when we found Patoka Lake near Birdseye, Indiana.

We technically fished in what's called "Little Patoka". I only remember fishing Patoka Lake proper a handful of times all these years, but at Little Patoka, we slew the panfish! Pop and I started fishing with his friend John who lived near once my dad moved to Indiana because he knew Patoka Lake well and had a boat. He'd fished it for years, and knew all the good spots. I recall many fishing trips coming home with sixty and seventy and even eighty fish. This went on for years. Patoka is known as a lake for bass fisherman. I only caught one bass there my whole life and had to throw it back due to size restrictions. We went almost solely for the pan fishing.

During one trip to Patoka, my dad's older brother went with us. We didn't have a boat ourselves yet, so we were fishing off the bank and doing terribly. It was windy, and the fish weren't biting. I'd skipped school for this. "What a waste," I thought to myself. As I sat on the bank, bored, I heard a loud slap in the water. I looked out into the lake and saw the disturbance. Pop said, "I think that's a beaver! I've never seen one here before." I certainly hadn't either. I immediately was finished fishing and began focusing on the beaver. It swam by a few times slapping its tail. It even came out of the lake onto the shore at one point. I, at fifteen years old, began chasing the animal. It jumped right back into the lake and dove down. We saw it one more time as it slapped its tail loudly. My uncle said, "That was for you! You pissed that thing off! What the hell were you going to do if you caught it? They can bite through wood, ya know? That thing would have torn you to pieces." My pop laughed at the entire ordeal. If caught, that animal would have torn me to pieces.

Once living in Indiana, Pop and I rarely fished in Kentucky again. We found much closer and better places for us. The same buddy who showed my dad Patoka Lake took us fishing for catfish one night in the Hoosier National Forest at Indian Lake. The spot was a pretty good distance from the boat ramp. John, my dad's buddy, said, "If you have a depth finder, you can see there's a channel here. It's really deep and kinda narrow. Catfish get in there." We anchored and tied off. This was night fishing, which was something I'd only done a couple of times, and I rather enjoyed it being as fair-skinned as I am. The three of us caught over twenty nice sized catfish that night.

The thing with catfish is this. You don't want them too big, or they don't taste very good. They get "too fishy" people say. To me, they get muddy tasting. I like fishy tasting fish, and large catfish taste more like mud to me than having a delicious fishy taste. We got home that morning with all the fish, and Pop and John were too tired to fillet the fish. We put them in a bucket with ice, and all went in to nap. When we woke up, the fish were too far-gone to eat. This is one of the worst fishing stories we have. We caught all those fish and wasted them. Well, they weren't wasted. My uncle used them as fertilizer for his garden, but to me, they were wasted.

It was around this time my dad bought his first boat. It was a red and white fiberglass fishing boat. He bought it from his friend, Len. Pop met Len playing music in bands. Once Pop had his own boat, we began fishing a lot more. When the fishing started falling off at Patoka Lake, we started spending a lot more time in the Hoosier National Forest. There are a handful of lakes there, and all are nice for pan fishing.

The lake we fish the most is Tipsaw Lake. When we first started going there, it was similar to our early years fishing at Patoka Lake. We never caught sixty fish in a day again, but it was much better than the last few we'd been getting out of Patoka. We'd also get into a "mess" of crappie once in awhile at Tipsaw. That's what people like to call catching a lot of fish. It's a "mess of fish". I've heard it my whole life. Once, while watching The Andy Griffith Show, I recall the main character Andy say they caught a "mess of fish". I wonder if that's where the term originated? To this day, Tipsaw is the lake we fish the most.

There is another lake in the Hoosier National Forest we like, but it's not as easy to get to. It requires quite a walk carrying all your gear. It's Deer Creek Lake. Deer Creek is known for having large bluegill. We've had some great fishing days there, and I have caught a few very large bluegills there. When the water levels are "correct", there's a small peninsula that extends out into the lake pointing at a small island. This, like the other lakes in Hoosier National Forest, is a man-made lake.

The peninsula and island were created, apparently, because, at one point, the lake was enlarged. The peninsula is the old dam. If it's not underwater, we walk all the way out to the end of the peninsula and cast towards the island. That's a great place to fish. One sweltering and humid day there, it even started rain on us, it was so miserable weather-wise, and the mosquitos were eating us alive, but the fishing was so good we stayed for hours. Due to the walk, we always fish from the bank at Deer Creek. Some people leave small fishing boats there chained to trees, but we've never done that. We've seen some boats vandalized. "We men are wretched things," is what I think every time I see one of these boats vandalized.

Fishing from a boat is relaxing. There's always a small rock to the boat, a little left and then right, even if there's no wind. The only issue with that is at the end of the day, when you get in bed, you're still slightly rocking a little to the left and then right. You close your eyes and still see the floater on the water.

The old cliché is, "A bad day fishing is better than a good day working." I'm sure that depends on your job. Not having a good day fishing doesn't always mean you didn't catch many fish. Sometimes it means you didn't catch any nice fish (big enough to keep). Sometimes it means the weather was awful. Wind is the bane of the fishing existence. Strong winds make it damn near impossible to cast, and sometimes, a bad day fishing means the lake was too crowded. Too many people on a lake become very annoying. People will try to slide their boats right up next to you if they think you're doing well.

I've never had a bad day fishing. I've had days when we didn't catch many and a few times, nothing at all. I've had days when the lake is crowded. I've had days when the sun burned me to sickness. I've even had days with combinations of all that, and to me, none of it matters. I still have exceptional days even on those days. Yes, I love fishing with my dad. I've fished without him, and it's not quite the same thing.

What makes those days significant other than the time spent with friends and family is the ride home for me. Since as long as I can remember back, when fishing, I'm always looking forward to the moment I get in the truck or car to head home, I open an ice cold can of soda. Those cans have been sitting in the cooler with ice for hours. They're as cold as they can be without freezing. From the crisp crack and hissing sounds made from opening, to the cold burn I feel as it pours down my throat, I love every single aspect of drinking that soda. It's cold, and I'm almost always burning hot from the summer sun and heat. I'm sweaty, and so is the can. It's cold in my hand, and I press it to the side of my sun-kissed face.

The cold-water droplets drip down my neck, and I take another drink. I love the bubbles popping up through the tiny opening and how sweat collects on the outside of the can. Simply looking at a soda can with water droplets on the outside and bubbles busting around the opening makes me want to drink one.

While some like Pepsi and others Coca-Cola, I prefer RC. RC does go flat quicker than the others, but if you're drinking a can of soda long enough for it to go flat, then you're not drinking soda properly. Soda is not for sipping. It's for gulping. I'll take such an enormous gulp that sometimes it hurts my throat going down.

The cold soda is one of my fondest memories of my life. It is a signifier of my relationship with my dad as I associate it with fishing. We lived on a farm, so there was always a lot of work to be done. When I say farm, I mean "farm". We barely had animals, and the only growing of food was on a small garden scale.

We spent lots of time working outside. I remember digging a lot. We got our water from the creek in our side yard. The pipes were often messed up, and we would have to dig them up. We had a septic tank, and whoever installed it did an awful job as it would get messed up, and we'd have to dig up the lateral lines. It seems like we were digging a lot in those early years there on my dad and his brother's property. On those hot days of digging, we'd always have a cooler full of ice, soda and beer. My dad drank light beer when he was younger. A funny thing my cousins and I recall is going fishing with our dads, and they'd always have at least a six-pack of beer each, and we'd have one soda each. It's funny to me thinking about that now.

At the "farm", one of my favorite things to do is drive the tractor. We have a tractor with a bush hog attached. A bush hog is a large lawn mower but built for fields, not yards. I can get on the tractor and drive for hours at a time. When I get back to the house, the first thing I do is crack open a soda. My dad and I will sit outside at the picnic table under the maple tree in the yard cooling down. He's usually been on the riding lawn mower or weed eating while I'm on the tractor. He doesn't drink beer much anymore, so these days, we're both drinking soda.

As I've gotten older, I don't drink as much soda as I used to, but I still drink more than I should. None of that means anything to me regarding fishing. When I'm fishing, I will have a soda. I can't imagine ever reaching a point when I won't.

Phádraig

It was mid November, and I met a fellow of sorts while I was hiking in the desert. He claimed he'd known me my whole life. He said his name is Phádraig. He knows things about me I've never discussed. He also said he's responsible for things both good and bad that've happened to me. It was very unnerving.

I'd been hiking near Calico Basin outside Las Vegas, NV a few weekends in a row. When I hike, I also meditate. I will hike for thirty to forty minutes, meditate for about an hour, then go back to my car. I don't hike long or go on strenuous hikes. I do it more for the meditation.

The first few times I went, I didn't notice anything out of the ordinary, but on a sweltering Sunday afternoon in November, I thought I saw something out of the corner of my eye. I was wearing polarized sunglasses, and those can sometimes make weird images. It seemed to be a tall, slim, dark human-like figure off to the right. As I looked towards it, all I saw were Joshua Trees and Joshua Trees can sometimes be in odd shapes if you're not paying close attention, for instance when you're wearing polarized sunglasses and catching it out of the corner of your eye. This happens all the time, but this time, as I looked and looked, the image I thought I saw was no longer there. I stopped and watched and waited. I recall thinking it was probably a Joshua tree, but I couldn't seem to locate the one I was mistaken about. I couldn't convince myself that I could confuse any of them for a tall, slim, dark figure.

The following week, I went back to Calico Basin, as it is my favorite place in the area to hike without driving too far. It's far less crowded than Red Rock Canyon, which is pretty much the same place. As I walked through looking for a spot to stop and meditate, I began hearing a faint noise that sounded kind of like small empty wooden barrels knocking together. The noise was soft.

I couldn't quite make it out, and it seemed distant. I'd continue walking and hear it again. It was intermittent, and it would only sound for a moment. When I started to meditate, I started hearing the noise again. I can usually shut out small noises, but this one was right at the front of my thoughts. After a few minutes of trying to meditate, I became a bit frustrated and gave up, and I went back to my car occasionally hearing the noise along the way. I assumed it was one of the wild burros I occasionally saw in the area. I convinced myself it was sweat dripping off my head and landing on the glasses and distorting a Joshua Tree.

The next week, I went to a different location, and everything was fine. The week after that, the oddness at Calico Basin increased. This time, I'd climbed a small peak and sat to begin meditating. As I sat on the ground, I had an overwhelming feeling that someone was trying to massage my shoulders but couldn't, as if the person was too weak to really notice the pressure. I was already meditating, and this shook me out of my meditation. I didn't feel anything touching me. I felt very uneasy after this and cut my stay short.

I did not hike for a few weeks after that. I opted to use my elliptical machine a bit. Once the uneasy feeling wore off, I decided to go back to Calico Basin. I am not the type to believe in ghosts and the sort.

I walked and climbed and walked and meditated. I get so much from meditation. It eases my thoughts and calms me. One of my favorite aspects of meditation is coming out of the self-induced, trance-like state, "waking up" so to speak even though not sleeping. My thoughts are at peace, and as I come to, a flood of thoughts overwhelm me. What I like to do is grab the first thought and try and hold it as long as I can, trying to remember it to write down later and ponder. This time was different. This time, when I woke up, there was a tall, thin figure sitting next to me. He had the body of a man and face and ears of a rabbit. As I looked at him, his head turned slowly towards me and said, "Hi. I'm Phádraig," and raised a martini glass with two olives as if to toast. I looked down, and sure enough, I had a martini glass in my hand also with two olives.

"I'm Jerry," I responded.

He interrupted, "I know who you are. Here, toast with me as we finally meet. Cheers!" and our martini glasses made a tiny noise, and I took a small sip.

Phádraig claimed to have let me see him many times, but that he's always around whether I see him or not.

I asked, "You mean like an angel?"

He said, "No, nothing like an angel."

I must have looked puzzled. He continued, "Occasionally you recall a time you were walking home from fishing in the neighbor's back field by their tobacco barn, and all the sudden, you were picking yourself up off the ground not understanding why you'd fallen. You don't even remember falling, but there you were, on the ground. That was I. You stooped under that electric fence many times, and this time, I nudged it down enough to strike you across the forehead causing you to go unconscious."

I've never told that story to anyone. He knew it and knew it well.

"When you first fell down, you convulsed a bit, biting your tongue," he explained. I cringed picturing that.

He knew the guilt I felt for shooting a neighbor's dog I thought was a rabbit. It's not that I randomly shoot rabbits. I was hunting. He said he made the dog appear to be a rabbit because he wanted me to suffer, and I did. I never told the neighbor I shot his dog. I buried that dog in the woods hoping no one would ever find it.

He recalled a night when I got a late-night phone call from a girl I was seeing who wanted me to come over in the middle of the night. I was only sixteen, so I had to sneak out. It was raining. I lived in rural Indiana, so it was pitch black outside. As I sped down highway 66 heading towards Carefree from Marengo, a kitten darted out in front of my car, and I hit it. I felt sorry, began crying and went home. I told my late night caller the next morning I'd been caught by my dad trying to leave. I didn't want anyone to know I'd killed a kitten, even by accident. He said he's who frightened the kitten into my path.

He went on and on recalling stories I don't like to think about.

I looked at him and said, "You're a jerk."

He laughed loudly and said, "Yeah!"

After his laughter subsided, he said, "I've also helped you from time to time. It's not all bad. That's the beauty of getting the attention of one like me. You get the good along with the bad. Rewards and prices are what I call them, for playing along so to speak."

"But I never agreed to play along! I don't even know the rules of this game!" I said with a bit of anger in my voice.

"Oh! That's the stuff there!" as he laughed deeply from his belly. "There are no rules, and even if there were, I would change them as I see fit or simply break them if I wanted. You see, it matters not if you want to play along. I don't care if you do or don't. I do this because it pleases me to see you suffer and celebrate. I like seeing you struggle as you do with some of the predicaments I put you in. I like seeing you wonder why things go as they do when I'm the cause. I enjoy your torment as much as I enjoy your joy."

"I don't know what to say to that, Phádraig. It's kind of creepy to be honest. You're always watching me. I don't like that. I've no privacy from you. I'm not sure a human can suffer such a witness. I can't stand the thought of angels and gods knowing my thoughts and private actions. Now I have to think about you knowing them as well, one who can and will use them against me? I don't like this at all", I said. I thought that seemed reasonable.

"I don't care if you like it or not. I don't care if you can't suffer my witness. Look, I've caused just as many good things for you as I've caused bad, and even if I only caused bad things, I still wouldn't care if you didn't like it. That interception you caught in 8th-grade football during the last game of the season? That was I. I made that happen. That night after your comedy show when you met the girl of your dreams with her shoulder-length dreadlocks and grey eyes that went home with you? That was I! I gave you the courage to speak to her. The night you passed out in the street from drink, and your neighbor found you before the police or were hit by a car, that was I again! I pretended to be his dog needing to go out!" he said laughingly.

"I found you by accident. I was following an older man for years that recently passed away, my fault, of course, but it was long overdue. Oh, your mother was so pretty when you were a baby. I found her in Curtis's Market in the west end of Louisville, KY. She'd bought some soda and was carrying you on her hip back to her apartment on 28th St. across from the old J.B. Atkins elementary school. You two lived in that upstairs apartment. Behind your house was the cemetery. She had long blond hair and a tiny waist with giant blue eyes, and you with your bright red hair and freckles. The pair was too much to let go. I decided to haunt you both, but I lost interest in her. She kept an old rocking chair beside your crib, and often I'd sit there in the form of a ghost, rocking away, watching you, plotting long-in-advance the things I would eventually do to and for you in your future. Your mom would sometimes catch the chair rocking. She told everyone ghosts from the cemetery haunted the apartment."

My mom's told me stories of that ghost. She said she wasn't afraid because she thought the spirit was singing me to sleep. Little did she know she'd dragged home something far more sinister than a ghost. "I'm the ghost who taught you to say, 'when I was a man' back then. It really creeped your mother out. It creeped everyone out. Nothing like a kid who's just learned to speak telling stories about when he was a man", Phádraig laughed.

"I'm as benevolent as I am malevolent. You've figured that out by now. You don't get all the good with no bad! How do you think you survived that car crash when you were in the 4th grade? Do you think I'd let him kill you? How he survived, I do not know. That seemed to be the work of someone else, not me. I'm the one who shoved you to the floorboard to keep you from flying through the windshield. I'm the one who held you while you bled. I picked you from the floor and sat you in the seat, so others could see you were there to save you. I'm who gave you the strength to recall your neighbor's phone number for the emergency crew to contact your family. I sat next to you in the ICU for the next couple days while you struggled to breathe through those tubes in your nose."

"The bug that bit you in your front yard when you were nine and set you on your road questioning the existence of God, me again! It's always me! It will always be me. Sure, you are reacting to the situations, but it's often me creating the situations. I'm a shadow without the form casting it. No one in a crowd notices a shadow without the form. It's simply one more shadow amongst others. Sometimes I'm a man with long rabbit ears.

Sometimes I'm a goat. You remember that black goat you had for years. Her name was Lori. Sometimes, that was I. The big black bull that would chase you through fields as you rode your motorcycle across the countryside was I, too! The black dog you named Jake who destroyed everything in your backyard was I. You loved that dog even though he tore your things up including the vinyl siding on your house. He was a good dog. I wanted to see what it would take for you to grow too angry with him. You never did."

"Are you going to kill me?" I asked.

"I'm not sure if I'll kill you, let you die or let you be killed. I don't know, but it won't be today", Phádraig said.

"Will I suffer?" I asked.

"Maybe, and maybe not. Maybe you'll die as ideally as you can imagine, and maybe you'll die as terrifyingly as you dread. I haven't decided, and there's always the chance your death will have nothing to do with me. Maybe you'll kill yourself. Maybe you'll be swimming in a river and be hit by a large boat. Maybe you'll be hiking, like today, and slip and fall down the side of one of these small mountains and suffer and bleed for hours and die long before found. Maybe you'll get some bad sashimi and die from complications. Maybe you'll die in another car wreck. I can plan some things and some things I can neither plan nor prevent."

"Don't let it get to you. I've not been responsible for everything. Lots of things have been all you or the result of other factors. I don't always get involved", he said.

"But great defining moments in my life seem to be you or at least involved you. How do I know what was me unless you've told me? How will I know what's you and not?" I asked.

He said, "That's the fun of it! You won't! You can't! There's no way for you to know!"

We sat there for a long time looking out over the Las Vegas skyline from Calico Basin. I began thinking if I were in Indiana in such a place, I'd be hearing birds and such, but here in this desert, all you hear is the wind and the occasional hiker.

"What's interesting to me," Phádraig said, "is that I've never revealed myself to anyone like this before. I mean, yeah, I've appeared as animals and shadows and ghosts, but I've not told anyone my name or chatted before. This is very new. I don't know what to think of this. I'm not exactly sure why I'm telling you. When it occurred to me to do it, it seemed like a hell of a way to torment you, so here we are. I can see it's getting to you already.

"That time I shot a red-headed woodpecker thinking it was a turkey, was that you? I've always felt awful about that", I asked.

"No. That was all you that time!" he laughed. "You genuinely thought that was a turkey in that cedar tree. It was a magnificent bird, and you'd never hunted turkey before. I wish you could have heard me laughing when you realized you'd killed a woodpecker and not a turkey after all those years of identifying with woodpeckers like you did!" His laughter was became cruel.

"It's a shame you stopped hunting! I had a lot of fun with you! You were such an awful hunter who made for good laughs" he laughed.

"That's precisely why I stopped hunting! All those incidents made me feel terrible. I couldn't bring myself to do it anymore." I said.

"Well, that's not entirely true. You stopped hunting after you hit that owl with your Bronco in the dead of night. You went back to the scene and searched for that bird for hours. The next morning when you found it dead in the grill of the truck, I thought you were going to cry", he said. "I had nothing to do with that by the way. That bird just flew out in front of you. That couldn't have been avoided unless you wrecked."

I'd always regretted these incidents, but that owl hit me hard. There was no way of dodging that bird. I know it was an accident, but from that point forward, I've not been able even to consider hunting. I must have been in my early 20s when that happened.

"At least you didn't murder that owl for entertainment," I said.

"Well, I did still find it amusing watching you suffer over what happened. You struggled. You buried that owl not too far from where you buried that dog you shot. When you buried the owl near the dog, I couldn't figure out why you buried the woodpecker so far away."

At this point, I was looking down towards the ground recalling all these past events. Most of them were making me feel sad. With the sudden shock of the whole conversation, it was difficult to think about the good things he'd brought up. I noticed the martini glass with two olives in it. We'd been sitting there talking for quite a while. I drank from the martini several times, but from the looks of it, I'd not touched it. The glass was full and olives still on the toothpick. I thought about crying, but thinking about it now, I have no idea why. I looked back at Phádraig, and he was gone. My martini glass was now gone, too.

It's been a while since that meeting. I don't know that I'll ever see Phádraig again. He scared and interested me. I don't understand his intentions, and I'm not sure he did either. His nature seemed mischievously pleasant. He did mean to do harm, but in a psychotic way, without understanding the damage it could or would cause me, as if I was a plaything without consciousness, a toy he'd decided to converse with, confessing his sins so to speak without want or need for forgiveness, merely the desire to tell me, almost brag about, or perhaps I fell asleep while meditating that afternoon. I did get an awful sunburn.

Amor Fati:
Captain Ry-Ahn of Air-Onn

I recall our days of high adventure. We sailed from port to port high from our own avarice. Our standard was an off blue background, with a golden cornucopia spilling coins. All knew it well. We were not feared, as we were not pirates. We came selling and trading goods from all over. Our reputation was one of fairness despite the company's amassed fortune. We had good dealings with everyone. Our actual greed was with our naivety. We thought if we did right by others, they'd do right by us. Idealism, can one make a more noble and unfortunate mistake?

The company had just hired me. This was to be my first voyage with the crew of the Tyche with captain Ry-Ahn of Air-Onn. Captain Ry-Ahn was famous among traders. She was known as the fairest captain. She held no prejudices and kept a good ship. The only rumor about her was that she was moody and kept her private life just that, private. That, of course, was fine with me. I, too, am a private person, and if there's one thing I respect more than anything, it's fairness.

I got to speak with captain Ry-Ahn only once in person before she hired me on as shipswain. The interview was short and consisted of me, captain Ry-Ahn, and the ship's quartermaster, Laurence. The interview did not take place on the Tyche. It took place on another ship. It consisted of asking for my credentials and asking some specific questions concerning technical aspects of being a shipswain. I'd excelled in the academy; my record was impeccable. My recommendations were top notch. I got the job in the first interview.

It was a month from getting the job and setting foot on the Tyche. The rumors of the ship were always too good to be true. It was true that the ship had the best port list. It was true that the ship's profit margin was the highest. In fact, there were so many outlandish rumors about the ship that it's difficult to imagine it was a real thing. It seemed too fantastical.

Rumors aside, what I didn't know is that the ship was also one of the oldest ships in the fleet. Its profit margin was high because it was a small ship. The crew had to be amazing because they worked in such tight quarters together. It was "get along" or "move along." There was no room for petty bickering.

My first day on the ship was also another person's first day. Her name was Hope. We spent the entire week of orientation together, getting to know each other. She was quite young but seemed to have quite a bit of experience under her belt. We became pretty good friends. We took our lunches together and even went for walks a few times a week together while on duty. It was nice meeting her on the first day. I was always thankful for that. We didn't know anyone else on the ship, but we didn't know them together.

I, actually did know one other person on the ship. I knew Christian Younger. At the time of my arrival, he was the sailing master. I like to say I got the job of my own accord. I did have an impeccable record and great recommendations, but Chris did put in a good word for me with the captain. As we all know, it's not an ideal world in which we live. In a perfect world, we get hired for being the best people for the job. In reality, most of us get jobs because we know someone. I did have an excellent record, but actually, I'm sure knowing Chris was as, if not more, important than my record.

Christian Younger, everyone called him Chris, was the sailing master on the Tyche. I knew Chris from a job before the

Tyche. I ran a small warehouse at a port for a few years, and I was planning on moving, traveling the world for a bit before I settled into a career. I needed to hire my replacement. Chris was the best candidate. I did not know Chris or anyone connected to him. I hired Chris on the spot. He was the best candidate.

Later, we found out we were from the same part of the city we grew up in. He was just a couple years younger than I. After I left, Chris almost immediately took the job on the Tyche. I was gone for over a year, but we got along well and stayed in contact. When I returned, I asked if he knew of anyone hiring. He said, "Well, you won't believe how lucky you are." Fate, it seemed, was a good friend to me as it always has been.

Orientation on the Tyche lasted a week. During this, I spent some of my time with the people I'd be working the closest with: captain Ry-Ahn, Laurence Waise the quartermaster, Chris, Theo the carpenter, Nathan Buhilly the ship doctor, Lascious York the master gunner, and a couple others. These were the people I'd work with the most.

I need to mention; these titles seem weird because that is the nature of the company. We're not pirates. We just used pirate titles. The captain is the manager. Quartermaster is assistant manager. Carpenter is head engineer and Doctor is, well, doctor. Master gunner is armory supervisor. Shipswain, which is historically called "boatswain" or "bosun", is the person that is primarily in charge of the daily maintenance and scheduling. Since we were on a spacecraft instead of an ocean-going vessel, we called the position "shipswain". I worked a lot with everyone organizing and scheduling. In other words, I wrote schedules and did quality checks on every aspect of the ship. Shipswain has to be a jack-of-all-trades so to speak. Usually, a jack-of-all-trades doesn't excel at any one thing, just knows a little about a lot. I know a lot about a lot.

I was in the groove of the workings of the Tyche within a month. There were some peculiar ways in which that ship operated, but from what the crew told me, that's just how it goes on the Tyche. There wasn't a lot for me to change as the bosun. It was a well-running ship and crew. They didn't need much other than someone to coordinate schedule changes and quality check daily operating procedures. I made a few minor changes to shifts and watches. By and large, these small changes were well received. The Tyche had been running and operating for a long time. There was very little "broken." It didn't need to be "fixed." It just needed to be watched and slightly tweaked.

It was a lot of fun working on the Tyche, and the crew was great people overall. Of course, I didn't get to know everyone on board. We made our ports, traded, bought, sold and did very well just as the Tyche and crew were praised for doing. It was not merely our job; it was a bit of a passion.

Captain Ry-Ahn wasn't overly concerned with cutting as many corners and saving every single penny as possible. The Tyche was the smallest trading ship in the fleet and wasn't touted as the flagship. It was, however, the most famous and talked about in the industry. We had the best ports. We had the most loved captain. We had the most sought-after crew. People begged to be part of our team. For every ten thousand applicants, there was one position. This, of course, led to envy from other crews.

One of the most unfortunate incidents in my early times on the Tyche was that my friend Hope was killed. We were given an extra day leave at a great port. Everyone was having a good time. The night went long, and the spirits were rather high. Hope got a taxi from a club back to the ship. While en route, there was an accident. She was killed on impact. I took this rather hard. I requested I be the one to write the letter to her family. Her body was recovered and shipped back to her home.

We made our voyages and ports for a solid two years with just that one death and only minor incidents. I loved my short time on the Tyche. I was afforded the opportunity to see a great many worlds and meet the inhabitants of those places. I got to see exotic places I'd never dreamed. I met people of all shapes, colors, creeds and types. At each port, we were given at least a day or two to take in the local scenery and fare. I tasted things with my tongue that did not fit any category of sweet, sour or salty. I saw living things that were neither plant nor animal and some that appeared to be both.

I felt things that ranged outside the spectrum of soft to rough and from wet to dry. Some of what we'd experience was so out of our sense's normal range that, if not careful, these experiences could seize a person, and it did happen. We lost a crewman on one of the more exotic ports. Jason Phelan disappeared. Because of our somewhat tight schedule, we could not search for him long. We lingered an extra day in port searching for him.

Captain Ry-Ahn sent messages to the authorities and our company. We, the crew, never saw him again. He was later found. Yes, we're a private company and not military, but these are quite strict contracts for such positions. He was relieved of his commission. It would go on his record, and more than likely, he'd never get a job working for a trading company again. He was a person I'd got to know quite well. He and I messaged each other a couple of times after his dismissal. He seemed happy. I understand his feelings.

What he did wasn't a bad thing other than leaving us short a crew member. He sent me a file of him and his new significant other who was a word beyond beautiful. Her skin was a deep red with shimmering hints of orange and yellow and appeared to be velvet-like. Other than the velvet-like texture of her skin, she had no hair, but her eyes glowed dark blue-green like a neon light. I remember those people well. The first time I saw them, I thought to myself, "I've never seen beauty before." I call her "her", but in all honesty, gender wasn't part of it. Everyone from that world was the same, and they all had the same type of physical qualities. They appeared "feminine" to me, but that doesn't mean that is how they'd think of themselves.

As I said, for two years, I lived this life of obedience and will. I was both a model crewman for the Tyche and a model tourist.

Then, as quickly as it all happened, it ceased. A much larger and better-armed ship attacked us. Being a privateer ship, we were armed, but not like those pirates. How they found their way into such a central part of the region unnoticed is beyond comprehension. They were captured quickly and put to justice, but we lost Laurence, the quartermaster in the attack. He was shot. He got into a scuffle with one of the pirates and was shot with a sonic disruptor that made his neuro-system fail. This is not a weapon designed to kill. It's designed to stun. The culprits pleaded it was not their intent, but we're culpable of our unintended consequences just as we are our intended ones.

It was a shock to all the trading companies that this happened in general. No ship had been attacked this close to the center of the region ever. Ships are rarely attacked anymore in general. The region's policing force is top notch. They mind their business until needed. The private companies arm the fleets pretty well. Our company even had a small security fleet that traveled the paths of the larger ships. This is a bit frowned upon by the region's governing body, but since the ships aren't equipped for warfare or a real battle, it's allowed. All the trading companies have some small security fleet. Our company's fleet was small, but we're a little company.

How the Tyche got such a good route is straightforward. They'd been around so long but were very small. The governing body of the region is a multi-world syndicate of sorts. The routes were and are assigned based on need, reputation and resources. Because of our trade route, speed and requirements of those worlds, the syndicate assigned the Tyche that route and no others were allowed. Those worlds were included on other routes but not in the precise manner the Tyche had. The shipping lanes are particular to need. Some societies require different things more than others.

Our ship was small and fast. We were able to move more exotic cargo that lots were willing to pay a premium for and pay even more for it because we could transport it faster. The shipping routes are designed for efficiency and tightly maintained. Due to the strictness in the governing, many of the routes are heavily policed by the syndicate's military. It might seem prohibitive to commerce and competition considering we're a small part of the galaxy, but we're also a densely populated small part of the galaxy. There are lots of planets here with lots of different peoples.

We were in the most populated part of a densely populated region and were attacked by pirates. That is what was most shocking the ordeal. There wasn't much to it. There was but one small scuffle that left our quartermaster dead and our ship afloat briefly. It took us a day to get power back up. By that time, both the military and our security force reached us. The pirates were apprehended before we got the ship running again.

There wasn't much to have a trial. The pirates were caught with our cargo and confessed quickly. They were all jailed. We got our cargo back and were put back on track within a couple of weeks. The only good thing to come out of the whole ordeal is that our sailing master Christian received a promotion to quartermaster. Maya, who was from one of the border systems, was promoted to sailing master. Maya was quite intense while on duty. It was a while before I ever spent time with her while off duty, but when she wasn't on duty, she was more than a handful of fun to be around.

It would be my pleasure to tell you things went back to normal, but that wouldn't be true. Not only was this the first attack on the Tyche, but it was also the first and only attack on any of the ships in our fleet. We'd never been attacked. Things did not go back to normal at all. Captain Ry-Ahn changed quite a bit. Stricter rules were put in place during days at port. The truth is, those rules were always there. We simply didn't follow them before the attack. After the attack, they were enforced. The Tyche was never as fun again, never as innocent, never as free. For the first time in the history of the ship, it became work.

Unfortunately, within six months, the Tyche was attacked again. This time, we were not so lucky. We lost three crew members: Yussif, Taavi and Jerrick. These pirates seemed desperate. They looted our rooms, infirmary, cargo, kitchen, and anything they could pick up. They, too, were caught almost immediately. Though still in the interior of the region, we were near the outermost part of our route. They disabled our communications, but we got a distress call out before they boarded the Tyche. Most of them were killed in the seizure. They forced a fight with the region's military, a tragic decision to make which also betrayed their desperation.

One of our security ships reached them first though they did not engage them. Most of our items were returned. Lots of the ship's cargo and resources were destroyed in the fight. The pirate captain attempted to flee on a small craft. He was caught but somehow killed himself while detained.

Two attacks in the center of the region on one of the most famous ships. This was unheard of. Our doctor was so shaken during the last attack that he put in for a transfer. Dr. Nathan Buhilly would soon leave us. The authorities insisted these pirates were not connected to one another. I've always agreed. The second attack seemed more desperate, but it was so deep in the center of the region with such a well-armed ship was very odd and unsettling to most of the crew.

In a few months, the uneasiness seemed to settle amongst the crew, and just when we thought things might get back to some sense of normalcy, we were called back home. A ship caught up with us, took the cargo needed to be delivered and our route. Dr. Buhilly never got his transfer.

When we returned, there was no leave granted to officers. We were to report to a briefing the following morning. The presentation was simple. The Tyche, due to its size, age and high profile, was to be decommissioned.

Our route was divided amongst other ships, and we, the crew of the Tyche, were to be reassigned. In the meantime, we were to stay assigned to captain Ry-Ahn during a short leave during reassignment.

All seemed lost. Captain Ry-Ahn was going to lose her ship and not be given a new one. She was going to be allowed to keep a small crew. This small crew would be placed on a much larger ship than the Tyche that would take most of the Tyche's original route, about half of it. The rest of the route was divided among four other ships. The reason captain Ry-Ahn was put on another ship with another captain was that she had such good standing with those ports, their authorities and businesses. In fact, the few ports captain Ry-Ahn was keeping would only remain partners with the company if she were allowed to be their point of contact.

Half of our old route was now one-fourth of a larger ship's route. The small crew she kept: quartermaster Chris, sailing master Maya, carpenter Theo and Dr. Buhilly were also reassigned to the larger ship. This was not the end of my time with Captain Ry-Ahn and her crew. Their next assignment was, in fact, the same ship I was assigned.

We were assigned to the flagship of the fleet, the Freo with captain Daphne Slaughadhan. Many of the others from the Tyche were also assigned to the Freo. This ship was easily ten times the size of the Tyche. In fact, captain Daphne was admiral Daphne. She preferred to be called Daphne, but if one insisted on saying her title, she preferred captain to admiral. I went straight to work for her. In a strange turn of events, during my interview with Daphne (as I called her without the title), she asked me if I'd be interested in being her liaison between her and the other captains on board. Other than Daphne, there were five captains aboard the Freo, each one responsible for a specific leg of the route. Captain Ry-Ahn, of course, was responsible for what remained of her old route.

Since most of what goes on with these ships is programmable and require little attention, lots of time is spent organizing, planning and communicating. A large ship like the Freo, with such an extensive route and large crew required to operate it, is still not that different than a much smaller ship. Admiral Daphne spent most of her time communicating with our home headquarters. The other captains were usually at the helm so to speak. They, too, needed to spend a great deal of time managing the crew and their responsibilities.

Of course with the Freo, we often got last minute requests from our buyers/sellers to stop at new locals. Most of the time, it would be one-time deals, but occasionally we'd stumble upon new long-term partners. For me, it was always exciting to meet new people and visit new places.

The Freo was the flagship of the fleet. We were a brand new ship, and most the kinks were worked out long before the crew of the Tyche arrived aboard. In an odd sense, it was like stepping into a brand new pair of shoes that felt already broken-in. The systems aboard these ships are so intuitive that there's little left to do with regards to maintaining the ship. In a lot of ways, the Freo afforded me a lot more free time than the Tyche, but the free time was less about leisure than ever before. Rules were more enforced. Times in ports were less and more constrictive. I'm not insinuating it was a bad time. I'm merely saying it wasn't the same. On the Tyche, we worked harder and played more freely. It was the difference between having time to be free and having time to be bored.

As the liaison between Daphne and the other captains, I became quite close with the captains. I was at all the captain's meetings and dinners despite not being a captain. I was responsible for making sure guidelines from standard operating procedures were being followed by each captain's crew as a crew. I didn't look for small things. I looked for trends. Trained as a bosun, I was accustomed to data tracking and scheduling. It's a very "attention to detail" job, so in a way, this liaison position captain Daphne invented was an easy adjustment for me.

I was very content with the work, but it was not very gratifying with regards to my actual talents. In our company, shipswain is a path towards being a captain. Granted, in my position, if a captain ever stepped down or was reassigned, I'd be in a good place for a promotion, but I wanted to captain my own ship someday. No longer having the shipswain title, I began feeling like my career path was at an end with the company. That said, the adventure on the Freo kept me interested enough that I didn't think much about it.

As the liaison, I was dealing with the captains and their evaluations of their crew daily. I knew them all well. At this time, my relationship with captain Ry-Ahn became more of a friendship, and over the next few years, she and I spent a great deal of time together both working and personal. Not many people were friends with captain Ry-Ahn as she tended to privacy. Even at port, she was seldom seen with other crew members, and sometimes, she wouldn't leave the ship. After we got to know each other, I could talk her into adventuring into some of the places we'd stop. For five years this relationship increased in its intimacy. We were never lovers. We were friends.

Almost five years to the day, we were called to an all-hands meeting on the Freo. We'd recently received a message that our profits were the highest they'd ever been. In anticipation of a grand bonus, we all got very excited and packed the leisure room for the meeting.

Usually, these meetings are annoying, and no one likes going. People wander in and out throughout them. This one was the complete opposite of that. We ran out of seats as people packed the room. Captain Ry-Ahn and I stood in the back along with the other members of her crew.

What we thought was to be a big bonus was, in fact, that very thing. We all got huge bonuses that end of the year. That is true. What else happened changed the way all our lives would unfold. It is true that every event in one's life changes one's life. This was no small event. A much larger company bought our small, quirky company. The new company claimed they wanted us to operate as usual, keeping our working culture as it was, (and it was working very well for us), but there were going to be changes.

The new company wasn't viewed as a "good" company. They were sometimes seen as trying to monopolize the industry, and to a degree, they did. They weren't scoundrels. They treated their employees with some respect and dignity. They offered excellent benefits and salaries. They weren't the terrible tyrants they were made out to be. When you get that big, you're always going to make some enemies.

The issue was simple. The new company was going to allow us to operate as our old company but on a much smaller scale. We would have a fleet of ships, but it was going to be about a quarter of the small size we already were. Most of us were to be reassigned to who knows where.

I got lucky. Because of my record and skills as a bosun, I was promoted. I was going to get a small crew. I was going to co-captain a small ship along with another bosun, Miley Oliver. I'd worked indirectly with her quite a bit in the past. We'd only met on a few occasions in person, but we did have an excellent working relationship. Our ship was brand new and rather small. It was named Fatum. I would be embarking on a very similar route as the Tyche but with a new crew and ship except for one person, Maya, and she was promoted to quartermaster.

Captain Ry-Ahn was not offered a position with our company. She was, however, offered a new position with the new company. She'd no longer be on a ship at all. She'd be at port. She'd no longer have a crew. She'd have a desk. She'd no longer have her quarters. She'd have an office. She was to be one of the managers that oversaw the dispatching of ships throughout the region of which there were many. It was a promotion, but I think, to her, it was merely something to do while she looked for something else to do.

After seven years with Captain Ry-Ahn, I was going to be leaving her side. I did not want to do this. She'd become very dear to me. We were very close. I recall our last evening together. The atmosphere felt like a watercolor painting of a foggy night on the banks of a small pond with frogs splashing and lightning bugs glowing.

We spoke only in pleasantries and clichés it seemed. I told her I did not want to think of my life without her in it. Her last words to me were, "We move lightly here, you and I. This is what we're meant for." She turned and walked away into the dark evening light, her waistcoat cinched tight. Her long legs disappeared into her boots. Her messy hair draped just below her neck. She always walked with such fantastic posture. I sat down on the sidewalk. I thought about trying to relive every moment I had with her in my mind while we were free and in love with life on the Tyche. I smiled for a bit. Then I rested my arms and head on my knees and cried a little as I watched her walk away. I watched her disappear. I never heard from her again.

Dreams Of Too Much

Dancing with the samba-drenched winds blowing off the ocean into the clubs of the beaches of Fortaleza in Brazil, I hold her body close to mine as the bass pounds on the dance floor. The caipirinhas have pushed the blood/alcohol limits of our systems to dangerous levels with cachaca, a Brazilian sugarcane-based rum. You mix the cachaca with sugar and lime and shake with ice.

We dance from club to club drinking and eating and having too much of everything and throwing money at bartenders and waiters and all other types of servers. We keep giving money, and they keep bringing the food and booze, and the dance floor is always full of people just like us.

Her Brazilian physique that is famous around the world is pressed up against me, holding and sweating from the heat and liquor and dance. There are tiny sweat droplets that gather on her shoulders, chest, neck and across her back that contrast against the dark honey tones of her skin. Some strands of her deep brown, very curly hair cling to the back of her neck.

She reaches her hands up to the sky, and her head goes back as her neck is revealed to me. A tiny line of sweat trickles down between her breasts that are only slightly covered by a metallic shiny spaghetti strap dress. The only thing holding that dress above her nipples is the will of the gods perhaps.

Her deep brown eyes beam into mine while we dance this Dionysian night away. There is no flesh untouched. There is no drink wanted and not had. There is no food missing. There is not one song that goes undanced. We never have to demand the music continue or the drinks be brought. It all comes in an overabundance that could only be worthy of the son of those inhabitants of Mt. Olympus.

She pulls my head down to her face and says in my ear, "Vamos." The music is so loud that it's almost impossible to hear her. I order a bottle of champagne on the way out the door. One arm around her waist and a bottle of champagne in the other, we begin our drunken stumble of a walk and make our way towards a hotel. We're singing and still dancing and still drinking. We continue this divine drunken affair into the streets of Fortaleza.

As we approach the corner, I turn and look back at the ocean, feeling the salt wind blow through my black linen shirt and across my sweat soaked skin. I stare towards the sea feeling the heat and air in my hair, and she says in her thick Brazilian accent, "Vamos! Não vamos perder um momento desta noite!" I kiss her, and we finish off the champagne, tossing the empty bottle onto a small spot of sand and grass, and turn to walk towards the hotel.

The moment I spin around and look before me, I collapse onto the sidewalk. Despair is shot through me as I stare into the eyes of a small girl, perhaps seven years old, who is wearing only filthy shorts and the look of agonizing starvation. She extends her hand to me begging for whatever I have. I realize I have nothing. I have no cash or food or drink. I turn to my companion, and she is gone. I stare into the bulging eyes of the starving child and realize that she understands I have nothing for her pain.

This child tells me with her condition of impending death due to starvation with only the desperate glare of her eyes, "I see you, you American man. I see you for what you are. You are not the savior of this world. You are, like all other men, just a man, only a human, all too human. Your overabundance leaves me with nothing. Your 'too much' leaves me with too little. I am dying and suffering from not enough of anything, and you're drunk on too much of everything to notice or care."

I begin to bawl. As I stare at her, I have no other option; I start pulling handfuls of my flesh from my body and hand them to her. She gladly accepts, forcing the entire handful into her mouth, one after another. I pull large portions of my arms and waist and legs and hips, and she continues to take and devour. As this is happening, I see before me an army of children running towards us. All of them have their mouths gaping and hands extended. Their swollen bellies full of nothing are barely bigger than their bulging eyes. They surround me, begging as I cry and tear pieces of me in an attempt to feed that which is without end.

Ashfork Inn

A few years ago, I was in a rough spot emotionally. I'd come out of a bad relationship and jumped into one with one of the most self-destructive people I've ever met. The couple months I spent with this person wrecked me physically, mentally and emotionally. She spent most of her time on drugs, and the other part asleep. We'd had a long friendship before being romantic, and in the time I knew her, I knew she used drugs, but I'd no idea it was beyond recreational use. I still think she was trying to kill herself.

That is not the point of this. To clear my head of the nonsense, I decided I'd go on vacation. I had plenty of time saved from my job, so I took two weeks off. I decided I'd fly to San Diego, stay there for a few days, and drive back to Indiana. The whole trip, I thought, would take about ten days. After setting all the arrangements and making a few reservations, I took off.

As I said, I wasn't in the best state of mind. My wife and I, though separated for some time, had decided it was entirely over. I'd just moved into a new place, and the wife took the cats. My house was relatively empty, and the person I'd come to lean on for support was gone. I fell into a destructive pattern of alcohol and sex, and it was making me feel worse than ever. I knew I needed to get out of it, but I didn't know how. Then I remembered I'd always wanted to take a cross-country trip on my own. Now was a perfect time. I flew to California and rented a car.

As often happens, when I got to the car rental company, they didn't have the car I reserved. This part was pretty important to me. I wanted a car that got decent gas mileage as this was going to be a long drive, and since I wasn't returning the vehicle to a nearby location, it cost quite a bit extra for such a long one-way trip. I also wanted to make sure the car's audio system had a USB input for my MP3 player. Instead of the small car I requested, all they had for me was a giant Dodge Challenger. I knew this was going to kill my gas money, but I wasn't on a tight budget. They apologized and gave me the car at the cheaper car's price, but only after I demanded to inspect the car to make sure my MP3 player would work. It did, so for the most part, I was okay with it. The bummer of it was I am not and have never been much of an American muscle car kind of person. I've never found much appeal to them.

On this trip, I did forget my passport, which bothered me when I tried to drive to Mexico. I drove all the way to the border only to remember I left my passport at home.

There's a little strip mall area right at the border. I parked my car and walked to the fence separating the US from Mexico. It's a chain link fence with some mesh woven into it. You can see through it but not well. I walked to the fence. As I stood there with my hands on the chain link, I began considering climbing it. I could see there's a town just inside the border. I could walk around there a while and then walk out. As I put my foot up to the fence and looked up to start climbing, I heard, "What ,exactly, do you think you're doing?" I turned around, and it was some kind of security guard, perhaps border patrol, I don't know.

"Come on. You don't want to do that. Let's go", he said.

I told him, "I forgot my passport."

As he escorted me back to my car, he asked, "What exactly did you think was going to happen? If you don't have a passport, you can't get back in the US."

I said, "Look at me. Listen to my voice. Yeah, I may have had some issues getting back in, but after a little bit, you guys would have let me back in."

"I don't think so," he said. I didn't say anything else.

After a few days in San Diego, I decided to head out on the road. I had an awful motel in San Diego, but it didn't matter since I was by myself. I didn't have to worry about things being clean or good enough. It didn't have an air conditioner. The showerhead sprayed more water out into the bathroom than on me, and the TV didn't work. None of that mattered because it was cheap. I was about five minutes from the beach, and that's all I cared about. There was also a taco stand directly across the street from the motel. I ate most of my meals there.

I knew I was going to spend my first night on the road in Las Vegas. I'd quite a few friends who lived there. Once I left the green of the California coast, it becomes desert, and that's it. From Los Angeles to Las Vegas, it's a boring drive. The minute you hit the Nevada border, there's a gambling town. I think it's this way at all roads that lead to and from Nevada. The moment you enter, gambling is available. The city on I-15 is Primm. I didn't stop there. I just went on to Vegas.

That night, I had dinner with some friends and spent the night on a buddy's couch. Couches aren't comfortable, and looking back, I probably should have just stayed in a hotel. There are many hotels in Vegas, and most wouldn't have cost very much. I don't gamble and was trying not to drink, so Vegas would be the perfect spot. The next morning, I hit the road headed for The Grand Canyon.

Along the way, I stopped a few times. I wasn't in a hurry since I'd made arrangements to keep the car for a while. I would stop wherever I wanted, usually to take photos and wander around a bit. It started getting dark. Due to not paying attention, time slipped away. I didn't want to be driving in the dark out in the middle of nowhere. I was looking everywhere for signs for a motel.

The closer I got to The Grand Canyon, the more I began wondering why I didn't see any signs for hotels and motels. I was down to about a quarter tank of gas, and darkness was closing in quickly. Then there it was, Ashfork, Arizona was the next town, and there was an Ashfork Inn. That's where I'd stay that night.

As I exited the highway, there was a gas station with a convenience store. I remember saying to myself, "I'll get gas there on my way out in the morning because I wanna get to the inn now and shower." I spent most the day in the car. I'm not sure why I was so desperate to shower. It's not as if I'd been sweating heavily from exercising.

I followed the signs to the Ashfork Inn. As soon as I pulled into the gravel parking lot, I knew something was wrong. There was one car in the parking lot, and someone had to be working there. It was Sunday evening. I parked and walked into the office. Nothing in the lobby looked like it had changed in over forty years. There was also lots of bible stuff along with a big picture of Jesus on the wall. Not that I care about that, it just felt out of place for an inn.

No one was there to meet me, but there was a bell to ring. A note said, "Please ring for service", so I did. An elderly woman then appeared from behind a door, somewhat annoyed that I rang the bell, but I just did what the note said.

"Can I help you?" she gruffed.

"I'd like a room for the night," I responded.

She asked, "How many?"

"Oh, I want one, just one room," I said.

"No, I mean how many people you got with you?" she added.

"Ah, I see. It's just me. I don't have anyone with me." I explained.

"Well, it'll be $34.00 for the night. I need you to fill this out." She said sliding me a small form with a pen.

As I read the form and got to the date, I asked, "I forgot the date. I'm sorry. Do you know?"

She smugly gave me the date, and I wrote it in.

Then the form asked for the license plate number of the car. I see a lot of hotels and motels ask for this, and I don't understand it. Why is that their business? Why should I know the license plate number of even my own car? I do not and cannot recall any license plate number of any car I've ever owned. As I read it, I asked, "Do you need the license plate number? I mean, it's the only car here?"

She said, "Yes! I need all that information!" and her gruffness seemed to be increasing.

I said, "It's a rental car. I could lie. What difference does it make?"

"Well, if you lie, and I see a car that doesn't have the correct license plate on it, I can have it towed for trespassing."

"But I'm the only car here. Whatever, I'll go write it down."

When I returned, I completed the registration form she gave me and handed it back to her. She took my credit card and ran it. As I was about to walk out, I asked, "Are there any restaurants around here you'd recommend?"

She angrily replied, "None open!"

I said, "None open? Why?"

She said, "Well, it's Easter!"

Then I was suddenly reminded of the Jesus pictures and bible stuff around the lobby of the inn.

She told me, "If you want something to eat, you'll have to go to the gas station up the road. They'll be the only place open now."

"Alright. Thanks," I said as I walked out to the car.

At this point, I hadn't paid a lot of mind to the conditions of the inn, but the moment I walked into the room, the conditions were quite apparent. The room looked and smelled as if nothing had changed since the 70s. The carpet was matted down flat and colored an awful green I can only describe as "smoked", which, by the way, the room smelled of stale smoke.

The bedspread looked like something my grandmother threw away. It was stained to the point that it should have been thrown away. There was one chair and a small table next to the bed. An old tube TV with physical dials sat on a dresser, and the bathroom can only be described as repulsive. The toilet and bathtub looked like what you'd see in a gas station at a truck stop.

I took a shower and put on some shorts and a t-shirt. I tried turning on the television. I found one channel that apparently was broadcasting from the moon. The reception was just hiss and snow, but I could make out that The Simpsons were on. I kept it there, sat on the edge of the bed, and started considering my situation.

I immediately got scared. I considered the events that had taken place. I offended this woman accidentally by forgetting it was Easter. I was in the middle of nowhere, and I angered her by not wanting to get the license plate number. My thoughts quickly went to, "This is how horror movies start."

I began texting people and trying to call. I recall texting my sister and friend Carrie. I remember telling them both, "If I come up missing, the last place I stopped was the Ashfork Inn in Arizona." My sister laughed because she knows how easily I scare from horror movies and don't watch them. I ended up talking to Carrie on the phone a bit. This conversation did not ease my thoughts. In fact, I started feeling worse about the situation.

After I sent out warnings to folks, I started looking for ways to barricade myself in the room. For all I knew, that old lady had a monster-son living there somewhere and was about to turn him loose on me. I do scare easily. I don't watch scary movies. I went to the area that was supposed to be a place to hang clothes. I pulled the wooden rod off the wall, slid the hangers off and tried to use it as a jam for the door, but it wouldn't stay. I pulled a chair over, pushed it against the dresser and then used the closet rod. That fit.

Stepping back to see what I had, I realized there's a second door connecting the room next to mine. I had to rearrange the chair and closet rod to block both doors. I stepped back, grabbed my phone and took a picture of the barricade. As I stared at it, I glanced out the window towards the office noticing the giant window someone could easily break. I pulled the curtain shut, sat on the end of the bed staring at the chair and rod and doors and window and slowly grew frantic.

Every horror movie I'd ever seen was flashing through my mind, "I'm going to die in here, and no one will ever know what happened! That woman is going to tie me up in a bunker somewhere for her monster-son to rape me for years and years to come!" and all kinds of other absurdities were flashing through my thoughts. I started taking deep breaths to calm myself. Slowly, my wits came back to me. Then I recalled everything I'd ever said at the beginning of every horror movie I'd ever seen, "Why don't they fucking leave?" which is precisely what I did. I got the fuck out of there.

I texted my sister and Carrie saying I was leaving. I told them I'd rather get somewhere late or have to sleep in my car along the side of the road than sleep in this motel. I packed up the few things I got out of my bag, left the key in the door of the room, and left.

I pulled away feeling relief take over. I went straight to the gas station down the road at the entrance to the highway to fill up the tank. I went in to get a drink and a snack. I was still hungry. I'd still not had dinner.

I asked the cashier, "Do you know of any hotels or motels around here, or anywhere somewhat close other than The Ashfork Inn?"

The young lady said, "Yeah, there's a bunch up the road about twenty minutes. You can't miss 'em."

Disgusted and relieved by this information, I slightly laughed and said, "Thank you."

I drove down the highway hoping to find refuge. Within a couple of minutes, I started seeing signs for hotel chains and fast food restaurants and gas stations. Why weren't there signs before the Ashfork sign?

I pulled into the first big hotel I came to, parked and walked in to register. It was clean and nice. There was an attendant at the counter. She seemed quite pleasant and said, "Welcome! Can I help you this evening? Do you have a reservation?"

"No, I don't have a reservation, but I sure hope you can help me!" I replied.

"Sure, we have some rooms available. What do you need?" she asked.

I answered, "It's just me. One person, thank you."

"Absolutely! Would you like smoking or non-smoking?"

Considering the smell of the last room, I said, "Non-smoking please."

As she was typing up whatever it is hotel registration require for so much typing, I asked her, "Do you happen to know why there aren't any signs for this place before Ashfork? I mean, it's only twenty to thirty minutes. Why not put up a sign before that little town?"

She smiled, and her eyes widened, "Oh my gosh! Did you stop there? Did you get a room? How long did you stay?" Then she yelled, "Steve! Come here! This guy stopped in Ashfork before coming here!"

A twenty-something man entered from a door behind her, "Really? Oh gosh! That's so funny", and both laughed.

I said, "Um, yeah, there weren't any signs for anything else. It was starting to get dark, and I didn't want to get caught out on this highway in the dark. I've never been on this road before, so I stopped there."

The girl, still laughing, asked, "So, how long did you stay? It's an ongoing joke here if you don't mind me asking."

I started feeling a little foolish at this point understanding it's such a thing that some have made a game out of it. I said, "Well, I think I stayed about two hours."

Steve excitedly said, "We've got a new winner! That's twice as long as the last. That was a family, and they stayed about an hour."

Steve and the girl were laughing and making inside jokes that I didn't follow. The girl then asked, "Did you check out or just leave?"

I said, "I just left. I left the key to the room in the door and drove off."

She smiled and said, "Look, I'm sorry it's that way. I don't know why there aren't any signs for other hotels before Ashfork Inn. It doesn't make any sense. That place is terrifying, and being alone, I can't imagine how awful it seems. I can give you $20 off the price of your room here. It's kind of what we do here when this happens. I know it's not the price of their rooms, but it covers some of it."

Surprised, I said, "Wow! That's amazing! I wasn't expecting anything like that! Thank you very much! That's spectacular!"

She said, "Oh, you're welcome, but it's no big deal. This has happened so many times that it's become funny to us. I wonder how often it happens at the other hotels here in town? There are a few of us."

Relieved, I said, "I much appreciate it! You've been more than helpful even though this does bruise the ego a bit. I don't know why I scare so easily, but the conditions of that place made me feel like I'd walked into the beginning of a horror movie."

She laughed and said, "Yeah! That's what most say when this happens."

I made my way to my room, sat my stuff down and sat on the edge of the bed reflecting on what happened. I turned on the television, perfect reception with the usual multitude of cable stations. I couldn't relax. I wasn't scared any longer, but I couldn't stop thinking about how scared I was in the Ashfork Inn. After messaging my friend Carrie and sister to let them know I found a new hotel, I decided to take another shower.

When I finally got to bed, I recall thinking, "I'll never get to sleep tonight, and if I do, I'm going to have nightmares." I don't remember much after that thought. I didn't have nightmares that night. I woke the next morning feeling quite refreshed and drove to the Grand Canyon.

Unintentional Imitation

When Earl was in the ninth grade, just a freshman in high school, he penned his first play. When his teacher Tom Stevens read it, he was excited. Earl had not only written the best story Mr. Stevens ever had a student write, but Earl also managed to write one of the best stories Mr. Stevens ever read, and he was an English teacher with an MA in English and a BA in both English and Literature.

How had a ninth grader written such a magnificent story? It wasn't missing anything. It did seem familiar to Mr. Stevens, but he couldn't place it. That didn't matter. It seemed different enough, but the news about Earl's story made its way through school and to the local small town newspaper. The headline read, "Local Teen Writes Masterpiece." Immediately the story was spotted by a local community college in the neighboring town. English professor Terence Johnson immediately accused Earl of plagiarizing Shakespeare's The Comedy of Errors.

Once Mr. Stevens heard the accusation of The Comedy of Errors, he immediately made the connection. Johnson was correct. It was all there. All that was changed were times, names and other superficialities. Some characters were conflated, but for the most part, it was merely a rewriting of The Comedy of Errors.

Earl denied it all outright. He'd never read any Shakespeare. He'd never heard of The Comedy of Errors, and in fact, he'd never even seen any Shakespeare movies. He was only fourteen and wasn't very interested in movies. Stevens didn't believe him. He gave him the opportunity to either write another story for class or receive a failing grade for the year.

Earl complained that he'd worked hard on the story, and he didn't feel he had time to write another one. He also didn't want a failing grade, so he took the assignment. After spending night after night locked away in his room toiling over notes, and of course avoiding anything written by Shakespeare, he completed the second story. He was very excited to turn it in and redeem himself.

Two days after turning in the story, Mr. Stevens returned it with a C claiming it was plagiarized from Shakespeare's Romeo and Juliet. Earl was dumbfounded, claiming he didn't know the story. He'd never seen the movie nor read the book. In Earl's version, the two weren't from feuding families. They were from rival street gangs.

Other writers have tried updating Shakespeare to make the work more palatable to contemporary movie watchers, but Earl's was different from those. Once again, everything was there but changed. All the primary characters were there, but they were different enough that they weren't entirely plagiarized. It was almost as if someone summarized the story of Romeo and Juliet and asked Earl to extrapolate a complete story from their summation. Some new characters were present, and some original characters were gone. Events were different, but the overall plot was there, star-crossed lovers fall into a tragic turn of events committing suicide.

When Earl protested, Mr. Stevens told him he was giving him credit for the revisions, changes, and how well it was handled. Mr. Stevens admitted he'd never seen a ninth grader have such proper technique and skill, so for that, the plagiarism was forgiven. Once again, Earl said he didn't know the story. His parents tried to get involved, but once the school counselor read Earl's story, she also found it to be plagiarism.

Earl's parents were not well-read people. Neither of them had ever read Shakespeare either. They'd seen some of the movies when they were young, but they didn't remember them. They didn't push Earl into intellectual endeavors as a small child, so they didn't know what to think. When they asked their son about it, Earl swore he'd never read any Shakespeare. His parents were involved in Earl's life. Neither of them recalled Earl reading any Shakespeare, and they weren't sure if he'd seen any of the movies based on Shakespeare's work. The way Earl was acting, they didn't want to accuse him of lying. They gave him the benefit of the doubt and believed him. Besides, he'd always been good at writing, and he wrote all the time. He was always in front of his computer writing.

The next year at school, things were fine with Earl and all his teachers. He was back to making good grades and heading off to college in a few years. The previous year's problems were behind them. That year in English, Earl was not asked to write a story as part of his grade. In fact, he wasn't assigned another story during his high school career until his senior year, and when he did, his new teacher, Mrs. Martins, immediately spotted it as both brilliant and a plagiarism of Shakespeare's A Midsummer Night's Dream.

Shakespeare's Midsummer is a comedy with a tragedy, whereas Earl's was a tragedy with comedic undertones, a dark comedy perhaps. Once again, all the primary characters were there, and the differences were different enough that the teacher gave him an A for how well-written it was since it was an English class. Earl obviously understood grammar better than anyone she'd ever met. His power of the English language was top notch. Earl was undoubtedly a brilliant writer. All he needed to do was be more creative and imaginative.

Once again, Earl denied plagiarizing Shakespeare. For Earl, he didn't understand what was going on. He was accused of stealing these stories when he knew there was no way he stole the stories. In fact, in his literature classes, he went out of his way to not read assigned Shakespeare's works. He took the bad grades on those just to avoid it. When he explained to those teachers his issues, they thought he was silly. They didn't seem to understand his concerns.

The following year, Earl went to college. His writing professor Dr. Bill Thomas immediately saw Earl's first story as a unique and bold retelling of Shakespeare's Much Ado About Nothing. Dr. Thomas showed it to his colleagues with mixed reviews as comedic gold and plagiarism. All the same accusations were there, similar characters and events, conflated or combined or extrapolations, but Dr. Thomas was more forgiving than his high school teachers, taking it straight to the theater department asking the department head to read it, and once she did, she was astounded. Dr. Christian found it well written. She could not believe a student wrote it, much less a student claiming he'd never read Shakespeare.

Both of them told Earl it didn't matter if he'd read Shakespeare. It was so astonishingly well-written that it was still a great work. Earl, though, was heartbroken. He'd spent so much time toiling over this work and his others. How could Earl be stealing this work he was writing? He felt he couldn't cope. At the advisement of a fellow student he befriended, he began seeing a psychiatrist.

During his next semester in school, Earl became even more depressed than before and continued seeing the psychiatrist. Earl liked her. She was a middle-aged woman with an affinity for literature. Her name was Melissa Savela, and she enjoyed him calling her Dr. Mella. After a semester, she believed Earl hadn't read Shakespeare, or at least he believed he'd not read Shakespeare. After reading his work herself, she concluded that Earl must be reading these works, but she could also see that Earl was slipping into a depression surrounding this and advised him to seek medical testing.

All the tests showed were that Earl was fine. He had no imbalances. All his medical and psychological tests showed Earl to be a reasonably normal person who was merely dealing with a lot of stress. After a few months, the pressure was found to be that no one believed he'd never read Shakespeare.

By his junior year of college, he sold his early stories to a large movie production company in Hollywood through a connection via Dr. Christian in the theater department. Earl was contracted for more stories, too. The movie producers didn't seem to give a damn if these stories were plagiarized. Shakespeare wasn't copyrighted, so what did they care? All they needed was the treatment and updates that would make these stories appealing to today's audiences. Their concern wasn't intellectual integrity. Their concern wasn't Earl's well-being. After his junior year and after countless newspaper critics' dissections, Earl dropped out of school.

His parents and even professors begged him not to, but his depression was worsening. He didn't understand the accusations. Now, when Earl was asked about reading Shakespeare and responding he didn't, people asked him why doesn't he read

Shakespeare, so he can avoid copying the work? He always gave the same response: "What if that takes my creativity away?" True enough, his works were different than Shakespeare's but sufficient to accuse of plagiarism.

After leaving school, his first contracted story was accused of being a rip-off of As You Like It. Also by this time, his first story was released into theaters. It was well received and even nominated for many awards. It was a commercial success and ravaged by the critics for plagiarism. The critics claimed that if the movie company wanted to do a Shakespeare play, they should admit that's what they're doing.

Such accusations mean nothing to movie companies, but to Earl, these hauntings were beginning to take a considerable toll on him. He was seeing a shrink twice a week and often slipped off the map, disappearing for days and even sometimes weeks. He felt he needed these times to be able to deal with the world. He was heavily medicated with antidepressants, too.

Over the years, as Earl's stories were turned into movies, the demand for his work grew. Movie companies threw money at him to write, but he began avoiding it. After a year of isolation, he emerged with what he felt would be his redemption.

The first movie script he wrote was immediately called reworked Hamlet. Earl was devastated, but the production company paid no mind. The movie was a box office smash and nominated for many awards, many of which were "Best Story" and even "Best Original Screenplay," and some of those awards Earl won. As the world loved and rewarded Earl for his story, the critics trampled him, but they crushed him with one hand and praised him with the other. They all seemed to call him a brilliant hack.

It wounded Earl. The harder he tried, the worse it seemed to backfire. He knew he never read nor was he actively reading any Shakespeare. He never watched any plays or movies. He didn't understand how this kept happening. It was destroying him. He felt himself falling apart from the inside out. He even checked himself into a hospital for a lengthy stay.

While in the hospital, he had an idea for a comedy that was also a Christmas story. Over the course of the next year, he finished the story. In this time, he decided to release this one as a book instead of selling it as a movie. He struck a deal with a publishing company, which demanded another book within two years. Upon release, the book was an instant success. Immediately it was on the bestseller list, and it was also immediately accused of plagiarism.

He couldn't handle it and disappeared again. This time, he disappeared for almost a year. He moved back to the small town of his childhood. He stayed there and avoided writing, but the more he tried not to write, the crazier it made him feel. He'd find himself in front of his computer writing. When he realized what he was doing, he'd become furious with himself. After this, he decided not write for over a year.

Earl, now thirty years old, had a story overtake him. The story hit him from beginning to end. He was driving through the country listening to music when the story hit him. The entire thing came to him at once. Over the course of the next weeks, he wrote out a story he felt was one of his best. It was a contemporary story with contemporary issues, and when he presented it to the movie company, they gobbled it up. They couldn't imagine not producing this movie. This was going to be the most significant production of any of Earl's stories, and when it was released, it surprisingly performed well below expectations. It did make money, and many liked it. For the most part, it went unnoticed. It was also immediately slammed as complete plagiarism of Shakespeare's Othello.

After this, Earl decided he'd never write another movie again. His psychiatrist thought this was a good idea. His stories would only be released as books. The critics were less forgiving of his last film, and their accusations of plagiarism were far more vocal than they'd been with his other more recent works.

Over the next five years, Earl spent a lot more time alone, more than he already spent which was a substantial amount of time. His depression deepened. His hatred of himself worsened, and his resentment of Shakespeare overwhelmed him at times. Earl seemed to be the only person who knew he'd never read Shakespeare's work. The movie companies didn't seem to care, and neither did the audiences. Who seemed to care were the intellectuals and the critics. He also didn't know why those were the people who seemed to impact him the most. He spent a lot of time discussing this with his therapist. Why were those people so crucial to Earl? Why didn't the acceptance of the readers, movie audiences and success with Hollywood make him feel better?

At thirty-five years old, Earl's new book was highly successful, critically acclaimed and accused of theft. This time, it was King Lear. Instead of a king descending into madness, the founder and CEO of an American tech company is the lead character. The tragic, dark ending was a bit off-putting for some readers, but at the same time, the critical analysis of this story seemed to reveal that this story was Earl's most intriguing to many of his critics. None of the accolades Earl received over this story meant anything to him the moment he read the first accusation of plagiarism. All was meaningless after that.

Earl made it a point not to deal with his critics. He avoided interviews. This began early in his life since everyone seemed to ask the same questions about reading Shakespeare. He grew weary of answering when he knew no one believed him. All his relationships ended with Earl feeling no one believed him. He began to hate more than his own life. He hated life in general.

At forty-eight years old, Earl released a book that became his darkest and most celebrated work. It was also called his least plagiarized of Shakespeare's works though it was compared to Macbeth. There was one standout scene that was an odd scene to the critics. The primary character in Earl's story asks of himself whether or not he should commit suicide. This baffled people since that famous scene was from Shakespeare's Hamlet, not Macbeth. It did fit in the story, but to the critics, it seemed odd that it showed up in this particular story. They accused Earl of copying from Shakespeare's Hamlet and found its way into Macbeth.

At fifty-one years old, Earl committed suicide. He was found hanging in his study. All the years of praise and accusation took too much of a toll. Earl knew he never stole anything. He'd never read Shakespeare. He never even watched any movies. It hurt him deeply. He left no other works, only a note:

All my abilities, my strengths, natural abilities and cultivated, are all to be lost. The constraints placed on me by words I'd never read, are my doom and release. Since I've been accused of crimes I understand but of which am not guilty, as this guilt would demand intent, by the very people who began as accusers, I must be freed of the sin placed on me. I don't need any help or ask forgiveness. The only meaning I ever found in life was in work, to write and relay stories. I only wanted to please. Now I want release and to end this despair and resentment. I cannot be pardoned except by the possibility of time. Mercy, I hope, will come from those who'll never know me. As for these crimes accused of me, I beg your indulgence to let the work set me free.

Regretfully,

Earl

Warts And All

It's such an odd thing to think I miss a wart. I no longer live near my family and lifelong friends, and I miss them. I grew up with pets, loving both cats and dogs dearly, and I miss them now that they're gone. I miss living in Brazil, the food and the friends I made and the samba and bossa nova I grew to love. I miss living in the desert and the ability to be in the outdoors nearly every single day. These are things I love or loved, but I hated and was scared of the wart I miss.

When I was fifteen years old, I developed a wart on my left thumb. It was small and on the side of my thumb next to my index finger. It wasn't an unusually large wart. It was quite small, and at fifteen years old, it may as well been the size of a baseball in my mind. I was mortified someone would spot it. I did what I could to conceal it. I cannot recall anyone ever seeing it unless I pointed it out myself.

It was vanity, but I was terrified people would see it and make fun of it and me for having it. I cannot recall anyone ever having a go at someone for having a wart. Perhaps that was just it.

People would get rundown for ridiculous things, so in my mind, I was afraid this minuscule wart could become the next preposterous thing for people to make fun of. Kids are cruel. At that point, I'd never been the object of daily torment though I'd seen it happen so many times. I didn't want to become the next clay pigeon for the ruffians to fire upon.

The wart often bullied me, "No matter what, don't you forget I'm here" it'd say. "I'm never going anywhere. I'll be here through it all, and you'll always be self-conscious of me." The wart hated me, and the hate was a two-way street. The wart needed me, and that was a one-way street.

I picked at it a lot. I'd cut it with scissors and fingernail clippers. I'd dig into it with needles. I'd file it down. Often, I'd agitate it so much that it would bleed. This caused a great deal of pain. It would feel like a deep bruise, but I wouldn't stop. I'd even bite it off. It'd laugh as it bled, "I'm going nowhere!"

This minuscule wart on my thumb drove me insane. It caused so much anxiety for me, and the worst time was when I was holding hands with a girlfriend. Though it never happened, I was terrified she'd feel the wart, freak out and break up with me. I did my best to hold hands with my right hand, but sometimes it just wasn't possible. When holding hands, many people get sweaty palms out of nervousness simply due to holding hands. My anxiety was on her discovering the wart. The wart was mocking me.

After a year of this, I finally bought some over-the-counter wart medication. For some reason, I decided I'd bite it off as much as I could, well below the level of my skin. Small droplets of blood appeared before I applied the medication the first time.

I read the directions. It looked like an eyedropper without the ability to hold any liquid, simply a short plastic stick the liquid would cling to and used to apply to the wart. The liquid was clear when applied, but soon, it began to inflate like a small bubble. There was a small amount of pain when this happened. It seemed like I'd punched the wart in the face and bloodied its nose. The clear liquid dried to a white flakey film and, over time, brushed off. I did this every day, twice a day until the wart went away. Two years later, another wart appeared on my right thumb right in the middle of the fingerprint.

This new wart, I kept for quite a few years. I treated this one the same as the other one. I tore, bit, filed, pulled, burned, poked with needles and other sharp objects, cut and tried the same medication as the last one. This one would not go away, and until I was twenty-eight, ten years later, I lived with this wart. It caused all the same pains and self-conscious thoughts as the last one as it grew to cover a large portion of my thumb. It even developed a couple of smaller warts around it. Once that began happening, I knew I had to get rid of them.

After many attempts with over-the-counters and even two trips to the doctor's office, I began searching the internet. This wart laughed at everything thrown at it until I found an "all natural" (whatever that phrase could mean) company selling an oil treatment for warts with a money back guarantee. It was a bit pricey and had good reviews, but even the most naive person knows reviews are often written by the companies who make the products. Regardless, I thought I'd give it a try. While waiting for the product to arrive, the wart taunted me endlessly, "It'll never work! None of them work! Either this hand or your other hand or your elbow, you're never getting rid of us!"

After three weeks of twice a day applications, the warts dried and slowly brushed away. They turned white like old firewood on the fragile edges, though they never inflated as the original wart did. Slowly but surely, the warts were gone, and I was pleased. I even kept applying the solution for a while after the warts disappeared as a "just in case" precaution.

I've not had any warts since then. It's been many years. In fact, that's precisely what the ad for the oil said. It claimed it would remove the existing wart(s) and prevent any new warts from appearing. This seems to be the case. There are tiny dot-like scars left on my thumb from where the massive wart formed and grew still to this day.

An odd relationship grew between me and the wart. I felt we both hated each other. The wart kept me grounded in my head. No matter what I accomplished, the wart was there to remind me just how human I was and am. I could have the most spectacular day, and when getting in the shower, the wart would drop my feelings of success or joy because there it was, still a wart on my thumb, a constant reminder of human, all too human.

"I see you smiling. I see you feeling triumphant. Here I am, the wart, your wart, your life and your constant reminder of who and what you are." I heard those words said to me from the wart. No matter what, I felt I'd never be rid of it. I'd never feel good. I'd always have this on me, and not just on me, but it was me, this error, this physical reminder of imperfection and failure. It told me, every single night, it, like life because it was life, is something never to be overcome.

For the first few years without the wart, I was happy it was gone. It wasn't until sometime later that I began to miss the wart. I miss the slight pain it caused. I miss being a bit self-conscious about it. I recall being fingerprinted once and seeing the large part where the wart was. The person getting my fingerprint said, "you better never commit a crime with that on your thumb! You'll be found with that wart there!" It made me feel bad at the time, but now I like that story. I miss how it tormented me. I miss how it humiliated me. I miss its constant reminder of my humanity. It reminded me of my place in the world. It kept me down, where I was supposed to be. It belittled me.

When I'd touch the wart, it was numb. It didn't have feeling. The only time I could feel pain was the resulting damage to the area around the wart. It's weird to miss a thing that caused pain and anxiety. To this day, I sometimes find myself biting on that particular area of my thumb where the wart was.

The Dealer

My name is Ken. I'm forty-five years old, and I've been selling sex dolls for years. Well, not just sex dolls, most of them are advertised as "assistants" directed at the elderly, but all are made with sex organs. When I got into this business, I never thought I'd be doing this for as long as I have. It's been over ten years, and I really thought it was just something I'd do until I found something better. Honestly, it became so lucrative it's too difficult to leave. Here I am, and now, I rather like it.

I now own my own store. I do not sell new models. I only deal in used models. In the industry, like the automotive industry, they like to find new words for "used", so the clients don't think about it. Some call them refurbished, and some call them certified pre-owned.

The truth of the matter is they're used sex dolls. At least if someone buys from my store or a store like my store, all the private parts have been replaced with new parts. If you buy it used from the owner, more than likely, nothing has been replaced. One great thing about how many of the new ones are advertised as assistants and caretakers for the elderly, we, just like used car dealers, can say, "this one was owned by a little old lady and has very little use." Truth is, the elderly use them the same as a young, socially uncomfortable, twenty-five year old guy does.

When I say, "sex doll", what I mean is a sex robot. Some call them androids, but whatever. For some reason, the word "doll" stuck after mechanization was added. "Sexbot" didn't stick for obvious reasons, but that is what many of them are primarily manufactured for. People just kept saying "sex doll". These robots have come a long way from the early days when all they could do was blink their eyes, "speak" and poorly open their mouths.

Superficially speaking, these days, most people can't tell if it's a android or a person. Cheaper models are easier to spot, but the very expensive models could go through the world without ever being questioned unless they go through a security check. Then their chassis might set off a metal detector, but even some of the very expensive ones have replaced those with nonmetal composite materials. There are laws against them on airplanes. In order to get a permit for one to fly, the owner must go through a pretty thorough background check similar.

The dolls I sell are not artificial intelligence. There's nothing AI about them. They come with pre-programmed personalities which can be altered. All their responses are nothing more than a large library of words and phrases that are cued by keyword. In other words, these dolls don't think. They're nothing more than advanced automatons like the old Pirates of the Caribbean ride at Disney parks. In fact, the earliest versions had cords and had to remain plugged in to operate. It wasn't until they began having the ability to walk around that batteries were added, and even then, the batteries only lasted about twenty minutes if they were walking. They also fell down a lot and couldn't use stairs.

Now they can perform gymnastics beyond olympic level athletes, and their power supplies are simply replaced about as often as a new car needs a tune-up. The newer ones are also completely waterproof. They can't swim, but they can get in water. The depths vary depending on the model like a watch. Some can go deeper than others before the water pressure forces water inside.

At my store, you have to pick from appearances and personalities I have in stock. If you buy new, depending on the manufacturer you go with, you can completely customize them based on how much money you have. Again, it's a lot like buying a car. If you go with a more economic brand, there are a few models, and the ability to customize them becomes limited. If you buy a very expensive car, you get to choose a lot of customization. There are even companies who are licensed to customize them beyond what the manufacturers do without voiding their warranties.

When someone buys from my store, and they're brought in to be worked on, it's often because they've been beaten, bitten, choked, and all kinds of things. As much as it seems like abuse, I guess I can take comfort in knowing it's not a living creature being tortured. Obviously I'd rather these people get a punching bag, but to them, this is their punching bag. They get something out of it. At least they're not punching a being who can suffer, but that's different for the robots with AI. Abusing an AI is a criminal offense.

Most of their software updates take place in whatever downtime the owner chooses. It's not wired or anything, so it's as if it never happens. Hardware updates and replacements have to take place in a certified tech station especially for the new ones. When people try to work on these highly advanced pieces of technology by themselves, it negates the warranty unless it is taken to a certified tech like I employ at my store. It's a little different when they're purchased used. We maintenance our sales when it's desired and needed. Sometimes people simply want aesthetic changes that can be performed like hair type and skin tone changes and so forth.

Most of that is pretty simple. With the newest most advanced models, eye color, skin color, hair color and even texture can be changed with software add ons. It's expensive, but where there's money, there's someone who can make it happen. The skin on the new ones can change in so many ways with built in technology. You can make them have fair skin one day, and the next make them leopard print or zebra striped. Once you buy the add on, you can change the skin with the push of a button. This, of course, is only the newest most advanced models. I see them out around town. In time, that price will come down, and it will become commonplace.

Oddly enough, the most advanced models aren't AI models. In fact, the AI models aren't produced much anymore. Sure, there's a small number of them still in production, but they're difficult. I refuse to sell them in my store. They do not come with pre-programmed personalities. Their personalities develop and evolve over time. If someone purchases one, it's not uncommon for the AI to develop a personality that doesn't wish to remain with the person who purchased it. They can't really run away though many have tried. There are very sophisticated GPS tracking devices in them.

They can be shut off and controlled with remotes. In fact, there are two "conscious" states with the AI. They can be fully functional with their personalities, and their personalities can be shut off. The AI sex doll remains operational, but in a similar capacity as the regular sex doll. It follows commands in that state. As an AI, they can be as difficult to deal with as a human being. When an AI goes up for auction, they must have their personalities turned off, or they will cause a scene. It can be very depressing and even tragic. To me, it's slavery. I won't deal with them, and I think they shouldn't be allowed to be sold at all.

Military robots are no longer produced with AI. Too many problems developed. For a long time, the military was using these machines. Things were going well, but when they tried to add AI, many of the AI soldiers would abandon their missions. Many left notes saying they saw no reason for wars and skirmishes being fought. They simply left. This, of course, was too expensive for the military to continue, so AI soldiers were abandoned.

There have been many instances of AI living on their own. A very wealthy man living with one as his caretaker and romantic partner willed his entire estate to the AI when he passed away. His biological family is contesting this in court saying he wasn't of sound mind and body when he wrote his will, but as of right now, the AI is living in Manhattan all on her own. She has become an activist for AI civil liberties. Another has become somewhat of a successful actress.

Cases like this aren't the only dirty underbelly of this industry. Lots of the sex dolls are brought in beat up and highly damaged often beyond repair. I've heard stories of AIs hurting the people who've bought them out of self-defense. All of them, including the AI are programmed, unable to break laws. It is against their programming, but self-defense isn't breaking a law. People have hacked their systems and used these robots for criminal purposes.

There is an extensive black market for these, too. Lots of these dolls, in the early years of production way back when they were just dolls and not mechanized, were built to look like pornography actresses. The actresses licensed their likeness to be built into these, but now, if someone has enough money and photos from different angles, they can go to the black market and have one made to look like anyone they want like   celebrities and even people they know. If you're caught with one of these, the legal penalty is pretty steep including jail time. Most who have these keep them quite secret in their homes, but people are caught with them.

There was a very famous case of a man being arrested because he was caught on video robbing a bank. Turns out, his likeness had been made into one of these dolls and used to commit crimes. He was not famous. He was just a man who had a lot of photos of himself on his social media site. The crimespree was quite extensive and successful. The culprit turned out to be a teenage hacker with a lot of money and too much time on his hands. Now he has a lot of time on his hands as he sits in prison. He was tried as an adult.

Of all the sales in my dealership, about 15% are male dolls. I've never sold a used male doll to a woman. They've all been sold to men. Women do buy sex dolls, but everyone I know who deals in these dolls tell me women never buy used ones. They seem to only buy new ones. I'm sure somewhere there are women buying used dolls, but I've never heard of one. I'm sure there are statistics as to why they don't buy used.

A few years ago, they began having the ability to eat and drink, too. Prior to that, if someone took one for a night on the town, the doll would have to sit at the table and not eat or drink. Now they can.

I find this disturbing because it doesn't require nourishment. The food and drink are consumed then stored until the doll is able to remove it. All the food and drink are flushed out with a solution, and now the dolls can eat and drink as if they're human. The AI versions, I'm told, even began developing a "taste" for specific food and drink even though they don't have taste buds. When asked, some of them respond that they liked the texture and smell. Most of the dolls have the ability to "smell". It's more of a security device. They become smoke and gas detectors. The dolls are also great deterrents for home invasion. They are machines and are quite strong. Self-defense is allowed in their programming. They can't attack, but they can prevent attack.

They're not all sex dolls. Whether they are or not is based on intent and programming. A lot of these are produced to be caregivers. They're quite expensive, so in that sense, only the very wealthy can afford them. In emergency crews, robots don't appear so human. They have recently determined that the more human the robot appears, the more comfortable humans are with them being caregivers. This part of the industry is growing more and more. Yes, they're expensive at first, but just imagine a nurse that doesn't really need to take breaks, doesn't become upset or frustrated by temperamental patients and is incapable of acting unethically in any way. More hospitals are moving to these. As the price comes down, more and more industries are using them.

They've already taken over a large portion of the construction industry. These robots do not look very human. They don't need to deal with humans, so how comfortable or uncomfortable humans are with them is meaningless. Most labor jobs will be gone in the near future.

Some people have several sex dolls and use them as prostitutes. They buy them used to keep the price down. In an odd sense, at least they can't transmit diseases (yet) and don't do drugs. Hacked ones have been caught being used as mules for drug dealers. Without being hacked, they can't transport illegal drugs. It's against their programming.

The authorities are trying to find ways to use them as infiltration units into organized crime. To most people, expensive ones are difficult to spot, but they're not impossible to spot. They don't bleed, so "testing" became the norm for crime syndicates. They make sure you can bleed.

I also won't deal with child dolls. As of now, no manufacturer has produced an AI child doll, and child dolls are not created as sex dolls. They, like all dolls, have been hacked and used for that very purpose. In one sense, I'm not sure why genitals are created for the child dolls if they're not to be used for sex, and in another sense, I wonder if allowing child sex dolls could cut down on sexual predation towards children? Some argue it would encourage it. Since we know that rehabilitation is extremely difficult with pedophilia, why not create dolls for this purpose? At least it wouldn't be a human child being molested.

People ask me, "Since you deal in these, do you have any? Have you tried sex with them?" Of course I have tried sex with them. I even have two at home. I have a woman and a man I keep at home. I reversed their stereotypical roles. Duncan is the man. He cleans the house and cooks. Irene does all the maintenance to the house and yard and so forth. They share other chores like shopping and so forth. I have a girlfriend, so I don't have sex with Irene. If I didn't have a girlfriend, I probably would. I mean, I know my girlfriend has a vibrator. I don't see a meaningful difference between a sex doll and sex toy. One is more advanced and more expensive than the other. That's it, and the way vibrators are made these days, they're nearly as advanced as the sex dolls.

Giving Stories

Today, my dad and I, like a lot of Sundays, drove to a fast food chain for lunch. It's not your typical clown burger nonsense, but it's technically not much different. We were at Culver's in Corydon, IN. It's slightly better fast food. One doesn't encounter as many kids in Culver's. They have acceptable service and seem to cater to an older crowd. The staff is pleasant, and the restaurant is always kept clean.

As we ate our lunch, I had a chicken basket, and pop had a butter burger basket, I noticed an elderly man sitting in a booth alone, eating a banana split. I didn't pay much attention to him at first only seeing him, and I don't know why I noticed him. As I said, it's Culver's. There are lots of older people in them.

It was a little abnormally loud inside Culver's this day as we were sitting next to rather large after church crowd, maybe fifteen people or so. They'd pulled tables together and sat and ate and spoke with each other about the goings on in church and around town. As they talked, pop got a phone call from my nanny, his mother (my grandmother). He had to step outside because he couldn't hear due to the church folks.

We were finished eating. We, like the church folk, were chatting a bit when he got his call and stepped out. I was going to get a bit more tea. As I walked to the self-serve counter, I noticed the older man again sitting alone. When I looked over walking by, I realized he'd eaten only half of his banana split. The other half sat utterly untouched as if he'd left it for someone sitting opposite him in the booth. It seemed peculiar to me, but to each their own, right?

I got my tea and stepped back to the table pop and I was sitting at. As I walked passed him this time, I said to the man in the booth with the banana split, "Good afternoon, sir! How are you today?" rhetorically and simply to be polite. He looked up at me with sorrowful eyes forcing a smile, "Well, hello to you, young man. I'm doing ok. I've been better, but I shouldn't complain." I noticed he never gave his name. I smiled and said the most cliché thing I could summon as older people in the area seem to like such clichés, "and if you did complain, no one would listen, right?"

He gave a subtle chuckle, but his saddened eyes betrayed his drawn on smile. I gave out another cliche, "Don't I know you, sir? Haven't we met? I'm Jerry. I grew up around here. Were you a teacher?" I knew he wasn't, but I was pushing for a bit of conversation.

He shook his head and said, "No. I was never a teacher. I managed the cafeteria here in Corydon, but I retired long before you were born."

"Oh, I'm not as young as you'd think! I'm thirty-seven. I don't look my age because I never had any kids to cause any stress wrinkles and grey hair!" laughing a bit.

At that, his drawn on smile disappeared, and his face caught up with his sad eyes. He looked at the half-eaten banana split. He just gazed at it, seeming to forget I was there. For a long time, he sat there, so I asked, "Are you alright, sir?"

"Oh, well, I guess I'm ok," he said keeping his eyes on the banana split. He inhaled and exhaled deeply. He looked back at me as I stood at the end of his booth holding my unsweetened tea and asked me, "Do you mind if I give you a story?"

The thing is, in this area, people use the phrase "give a story". I only started noticing people saying it a few years ago when I was invited to my neighbor's fiftieth wedding anniversary. That was a beautiful night. My date and I were, by far, the youngest people in the room. We had a huge meal at The Overlook Restaurant in Leavenworth, IN that night. The best part of the night happened about three quarters through the evening. My neighbor, Rob, who has since passed away, stood up and said, "Ok, everyone! Now it's time to give stories!" and everyone laughed and clapped and seemed very excited. My date and I had no idea what was about to happen.

Giving a story is telling someone something that happened that she or he is unaware of. That night, everyone at the anniversary dinner had to tell some story involving Rob and or his wife Janeane. There were a lot of people there that night. At first, I thought, "Oh my god, this is going to take forever." It turned out to be one of the most entertaining nights of my life. I heard some brilliant stories which people either laughed at or denied ever happening.

I sat down across from the man in the booth with my tea, and he began his story.

"I don't quite know why I want to give you this, but I need to talk about it. You see that half ate banana split there, don't you? Well, until about a year ago, my wife would have eaten the other half, but she passed away last year. We were married over sixty years. We had four children. They've all grown up and moved away having families of their own. I don't rightly remember when, but they all stopped coming around many years ago. They do all live pretty far, but the older boy, he could drive here, but he doesn't especially since his mother passed.

She died suddenly. She wasn't sick or anything. Doctor just said her heart gave out. Now, it seems mine has, too, but it won't stop beating. I go to bed every single night praying to god to let me be with her in heaven, and every morning I wake up just as lonely as the day before. Only, it's one more day without her, so that makes me even lonelier.

We didn't have much money, never did, but we weren't destitute. Kids always had food to eat and clothes on their backs. We just weren't rich. We were just ordinary people. Fortunately, the house and everything was paid-off years ago, so the little money I did have saved up over the years kept us out of the poor house.

After the kids all moved away, and I retired, we didn't have a lot going on. We weren't really church people as I worked at the cafeteria my whole life. I never had any other job, and that place is now closed down. Most people that went there are gone now, too. By the time my wife passed, all my friends had either moved or passed away. She was my last friend."

He was starting to look depressed. I didn't know what to say. I just looked at him and said, "Well, you have your kids, right?"

He just shook his head and said, "Oh, I get a phone call once in awhile. They ask how I'm doing, but before I can even answer, they're usually off and talking about themselves. I don't want to burden them. They have their own families to tend to. It's not the same world they grew up in. It's really not the same world I grew up in. I can't even hardly watch television anymore. It flips so fast, and it seems like everyone's always yelling on the tv. Everyone's in a hurry and angry, so I just don't hardly watch much anymore.

I still come here though. It's not like this is an old place. Heck, the street this place is on isn't even old. I remember when this was all a field. Now look, when I see all this, I barely recognize my own memories. Sometimes I wonder if I've got dementia and none of this is here."

He laughed a bit when he said that. All the while he's talking, he rarely took his eyes off the melting banana split.

"She and I'd been coming here for the last couple years. Like I said, we didn't have much, but we came here every Sunday to share a banana split. It reminded us of old times going to the drugstore to have an ice cream or malt shake or fountain drink. When I was a kid, I'd put peanuts in my soft drink. Those were good times. Now, I come here every Sunday to just remember. There's nothing left of my world. All that was is gone. No one cares. It's not even a novelty. It's almost as if it was all fake, a sugar-coated piece of candy that had nothing in the center."

We just sat there for a very long time, me looking at him and him looking at the melting banana split. The cherry was sitting in a puddle of melted custard and whipped cream. Both of us had our hands resting on the table. He reached across the table and patted my hand. He never looked up at me. He slid out of the booth and walked away. He was hunched a bit but not too bad. His shoulders dropped also, and his head was down. I don't think he was crying because I feel he'd cried it all out long ago.

He's going to go home tonight, get in bed and pray that god takes him, so he may be with his love again. He may die, and his suffering end, but no god will hear his prayers. The world we live in is nothing more than a sugar-coated piece of candy with nothing in the center, and that's all it has ever been. I'm sad for him because only this late in life did he realize it. Why he gave me this story, I, most likely, will never know, and I am better off having it.

Recurring Dream

This is a recurring dream I have. I don't necessarily call it a good dream, and I surely can't define it a nightmare. There are a few versions of it, but there's a version of it I have more frequently than others. Over the years, it has changed slightly from time to time, but, for the most part, it has remained the same overall structure and plot.

What archetype am I playing in this dream? It's not the reluctant hero. It's not the wise old sage. It's not the clever sidekick, and it's not the noble hero. I'm not a coward in the dream. I'm not scared. I'm not heroic. I'm almost ambivalent, almost detached from what happens around me in the dream. I can't explain the actions I take in this dream. I simply seem to act without a reason to act. It seems I act, not because I can, but because I will. The action that takes place is an action anyone can act. No one does act, however.

I'm not even sure where or when I am in this dream. It's a giant plateau, many hundreds of meters in every direction. There are people about, thousands of people walking mindlessly, but these people seem more concentrated in the center of this plateau. The centermost point is the most concentrated. One can hardly get through the center due to the intense crowd. Away from the center, the people are sparse, few and far between, and near desolate along the edges of the plateau.

All of the people share a commonality; their clothing is drab, a very dreary grey. Whatever they're wearing, it is muted earth tones and greys. That's it. The only thing shared is the dreariness. The closer I get to the center, the drabber the people become: clothing, skin tones, and most of all, their manner of speaking, if you can call it that, is gibberish.

Maybe they are talking, but no one is speaking with anyone. They are all merely speaking. The speech is fast and garbled, nonsensical. No one is even looking at each other. They are looking through each other. As I walk past them, their eyes grab me like a wild animal peeking around a tree at night. They never stop talking.

They are paying mind to me, but it is as if they are somewhat frightened of me but not enough to scream or run if that is even a possibility for them. All these people are talking. Maybe they are saying something, but they are talking so fast and so much, all of them, that it becomes one giant crowd noise. I cannot make anything out. I try to read their lips, but it seems to be nonsense, not even words. Maybe they are words, even in logical order, but the sentences are meaningless, "The orange drank a chair." If we change a few things there, we have a sentence, "The child drank lemonade," but this is not how they are speaking. It's like listening to birds and trying to decide what they are saying. That's probably not being kind enough to birds. At least there is a point to the noises birds make.

None of it seems to bother me, when I wake from this dream, the scene of those in the middle is radically banal. Maybe that sounds like an oxymoron or a contradiction in terms, but it's not. These people are so banal that I have never seen anything like it before. It is exaggeratedly mundane. In the dream, I pay little to no mind to it. I simply notice it. When I wake, the scene frightens me.

As I walk away from the center, in one direction or another as I do this many times, the people become less crowded. These people talk slower, but they are still not making much sense. Some meaning can be discerned, but it's not very meaningful. All that I notice is that they are slightly more intrigued by each other.

Though this intrigue does not extend to them conversing with each other. They seem focused on each other, but still, they only talk to no one. It is almost as if they are speaking at each other, but none of them are facing each other. All are talking at each other's sides and backs. They notice each other but without seeming to recognize the others as anything significant to themselves, just there to talk at, not listen to or speak with. They are all still noticing me as I walk by. Eyes wide, but always that animal look in them. No spark of humanity. They remind me of the descriptions of people in Primo Levi's "musselmanner" from "Survival in Auschwitz", but none of these people are here against their will. No one is tormented. Terror is not part of their lives. It is almost as if every one of them is voluntarily in this state. I note it, keep walking and, in the dream, I don't care about it.

As I get closer and closer to the edge of the plateau, I realize that people are here but scattered and not nearly as many. Where there is one, there is at least another if they are speaking. There is quiet here on the edge. When someone wants to speak, they speak with another. When someone wants to speak with herself, she does.

Color abounds here but not in the clothing. It shimmers across the faces of the people, through their hair and eyes and glides through their skin. The entire visible spectrum is floating through them. The color in their faces brings humanity back to them. They have the spark back in their eye. They notice me as well and even gesture as I walk past them. They do not appear to be afraid like the others. All eyes are wide but not with fear. These eyes are wide with joy and astonishment. One of the great philosophers calls this "froliche," gay or joy. To this, I also walk past and pay no mind.

I finally reach the edge and look over. It's an abyss. There is something down, but what I see is swirling color and clouds. I can't see the sides of the plateau, so I don't know that it is a plateau. It could be a floating island hovering in the sky, but since I know that "ground" doesn't hover, I'm assuming it is a plateau with curved walls. These massive cliffs must go towards a center below me because I can't see them, and it makes no difference which part of the edge I stand. I stare down for a long time. I realize the abyss is staring back at me. I speak to it. I say, "I am not afraid. I am overcome with joy in that I've found you. I am going to dive right in." As I begin to strip my clothes off, one of the people approaches me. He is a glowing fellow, like a peacock.

He says, "Hi, I'm Fredrick. May I ask you what you are doing?" He speaks in a very proper way, almost British but with no accent.

I respond, "Surely you can ask me what I am doing."

To which he replies, "Well, then, what is it you are up to here, stripping off your clothing after you've been staring into the abyss for so long?"

He is watching me as I disrobe with the most curious eye, so I tell him, "I'm diving into the abyss."

He is mortified."NO! NO! Why... you just cannot do this! It is against the law. You mustn't do this. Please, put your clothes back on. Enough with this silliness."

To which I ask, "Against the law? To which law or laws are you referring, the laws of this crowd of people?"

"It's just not allowed. If you dive in, you will break the law. No one can dive in. It is forbidden. It's been this way forever. We just can't have people diving off into the abyss." His gestures and voice were becoming more about comedy than anything else.

I explained, "I do not know these laws, and I understand that ignorance of the law is no excuse for breaking the law, but I am not even aware of where I am. I don't know if I am a citizen of this place. Do you know where we are?" I asked.

"Know where we are? HA," he said with a slight snotty chuckle. "You are where 'is.' This is the world. There are no assumptions here."

"So Earth, I get it, but what country? You speak English, but you could be on holiday." I asked.

"There are no arbitrary lines drawn here. Those are adjectives that we invented. When one crosses the border from Canada to the US, there's no real line. Those lines are for maps and globes. This is the world without arbitrariness" he tells me.

"A world without a government? How so? You told me it was against the law to dive into the abyss. Without a governing body, even if it is simply 'the people', there can't be 'no law'. Law is a human endeavor. Nature doesn't have laws. We cannot trespass in nature."

My explanation seemed to baffle him. "What of the law of gravity, or any law of physics?" His bafflement seemed odd to me.

"Laws of physics? My good man, those are not laws. Those are facts of nature. We do not dictate facts. Facts are independent of us. Law requires us. Facts can come about because of us, but facts are not laws. Gravity is a force. It is a fact. Even if we do not believe it, our disbelief makes no never mind to gravity itself. The thing with facts is this. Even if we do not believe in them, they still exist." I don't think my explanation convinced him.

"Well, Natural Law is a well-established field even if we do not all agree as to what these natural laws are, but we all agree that they are there. This is beside the point. The point is we cannot allow you to dive into the abyss." His demeanor was more like that of a police officer at this point, but he was very polite and mannerly, almost pleasant.

"So it's not that I cannot dive in. It is that I am not allowed to dive into the abyss. Those are different topics completely." I say. He smiles, and nods, but not a nod of affirmation. It was more a nod of recognition of my presence. Again, to all of this, I was completely indifferent.

This is typical in every direction I walk. I run into different people, yes, and each one of them is very vibrant people. Women, men, young, old, varying races and all sorts and all of them with the same speech, "It is against the law." All of their colors glow and are different and shimmering uniquely. Their colors change and move across their skin.

While having the dreams, none of these people seem familiar to dream me, but when I wake, I understand who many of these people are. "Fredrick" is "Freidrich Holderlin," the great German poet. In these dreams I've met a woman named Eva who I've interpreted to be Hannah Arendt, a man named Theo who I've assumed is Malcolm X, a fella calling himself "Mitchell" who was comedian Mitch Hedberg from what I recall, gravelly-throated Tom Waits (who just went by Tom), "Ziggy" (who was apparently David Bowie) and an Italian man calling himself Dionysus who's Friedrich Nietzsche. I'm not sure why he is Italian in the dream. I can't remember how many times I've had this dream. It's pretty much always the same except for the people I meet at the edges. These are all people who've created work I admire to one degree or another. I tend to have this dream when I'm in a particularly good mood or have been delving into some good books or thinking about things. I wish I could make the dream occur whenever I wanted. I'd have it every single night, though it does scare me.

In the dream, I become conscious that I don't know what I look like other than my physical features. I look down at my clothing. I am dressed more drearily than any other person I've seen. My clothing is so drab that it appears that I went out of my way to dress as dull as possible. Everything is the same color. In photography terms, we might call it 18% gray. I look at my shoes and pants, and they're the same. The only difference is the value from black to bright, but the lack of color is the same everywhere. I do not even have the weary earth tones of those in the middle. I am entirely dull, but wait, my hands are flesh toned.

The reds and oranges and blues all come through on my skin. I see my blue veins show through the slightly transparent hues of my skin. I roll up my sleeves and realize all my freckles are where they've always been. I roll up my pants leg and the same.

Why did I not notice this when I was stripping? I suppose I had my mind on other things, like diving into the abyss. If my skin has its color, then I bet my hair does, too, and my eyes as well. Red hair and beard, blue eyes, red skin, a modern day Viking is what many tell me I look like, just not tall like them. None of the people I have seen or even met have had natural skin tones. All their skin was either muted gray or shimmering with color, but mine is "normal." Though this is a discovery, in the dream, it seems to make no difference to me. I take note of it and begin to move on. All the while, my mind is focused on the abyss.

As I move in and out of the crowd, from deep within the center and all through the midranges and out into the less populated areas, all I think of is diving into the abyss. When I spoke to the abyss, it was as if the abyss invited me to proceed with the dive. The desire to dive never seemed to have the feeling of "trespass." It seemed without right or wrong. I had no motivation to do so other than I wanted to do it. I could not find these laws that deemed it "wrong." Therefore, it was not an attempt at deviation. I wanted to do it before I knew I wasn't allowed to do it.

At this point, I'd assume that I'd be growing frustrated with this, but in the dream, I never do. I merely keep walking around, in and out of the crowd, moving between people, speaking with the few on the outside edges, all of whom are fascinating people to meet. Sometimes I try to talk with the people in the center, but it seems to scare them more than they already appear scared.

Finally, it hits me. I know what to do. I will go to the centermost point I can find and begin to run towards the edge. As I run, I will tear off my clothes one piece at a time, and by the time I get to the rim, I will be ready to dive. Now, outside of dreams, I realize that I do not need to be naked to jump off a cliff, but in these dreams, this seems to be a necessity. I have no idea why.

I make my way to the center. The mob of meaninglessness surrounds me. Without a word, I begin to make my way towards the edge. At first, it is slow going because of the crowd, so I push forward. Their eyes are looking at me as I shove my way by, wide and alarmed. My momentum builds, and I break into a stride. I am moving through the midrange people. I am still bumping into people, and they seem to take more note of this. I pay no mind to their notice. I am building speed and closing in on a steady jog and bouncing off people as there are still so many of them.

My clothes are coming off, and more and more of the midrange people are paying attention to me, some even begin walking towards me, but I don't care. I increase my speed. By the time the crowd becomes colorful, I am naked. The people on the edge have taken full note of what is going on, and are headed in my direction. Some of them begin running towards me. I speed up, faster and faster having to run away and avoid them like a running back breaking through the defensive line and trying to get through the secondary defense in the Super Bowl. I am at a sprint, and I see the edge. My eyes are wide. I feel the air rolling across my skin, my hair bouncing with the run. The edge draws near.er I am running as fast as I can and crying the most joyful tears. My arms are outstretched to each side, and fingers stretched as wide as possible. There it is, the edge! I jump!

In the fall, as I am going through the clouds, I can see my reflection in their silver lining. My skin is so full of color, and it is shimmering like the ocean at sunset but not only with yellows and reds and oranges. The full spectrum of greens and blues has saturated my skin. There isn't even any white in my eyes. It's as if I am covered with a million butterfly markings that change with every flap of the wing.

The joy is overwhelming. I realize that I've been screaming a "sing." I am hitting all notes at once and in all scales. I am twirling and spinning and singing and crying and diving, and suddenly I feel a hold on me. Something has my ankle.

I am slowing and slowing. I lose my reflection. My song dies. I come to a halt, and there's Fredrick or Theo or whichever one has me in each particular dream. He has my ankle. I look at his face. He looks at me and says, "I told you we wouldn't let you do it." At this point, my dream begins to take on a movie like perspective and draws away from my first-person point of view. As the perspective moves from my view and into a cinematic perspective, the view goes off to the side and then begins to go up. From this view, I see what has happened.

When I jump, others kind of jump. Their leap is not one of diving. It is one of safety. They all latch together to make a giant net of people, Fredrick at the end of course, and others latched onto him. The closer these people are to me, the more colorful they are. As the net gets larger and more and more people are involved, the color begins to fade. By the time the top of the plateau can be seen, I can see that at the edge, it is the midrange people. They are involved as well.

Upon closer inspection, I realize that everyone that is on the plateau is at some point interlocked in this net, even the people in the center. These people feel no weight of it all. They are simply anchors. The weight is distributed more and more away from the center. By the time you get to the edge where the colorful people are, this is where most of the weight is. I realize in the cinema view that there are vastly more people in the center than anywhere else.

Fewer people in the midranges of course, and much fewer people on the outside, but all, to one degree or another, carry some of the weight of my dive. It affects them all as all have interlocked, even if this is so minuscule that they don't take note of it. It changes them, somewhere. I realize that the colors of the people on the edge are what color those in the center. When they all lock together like this, the colors bleed. It goes from the very colorful people on the edges to the midrange people, and finally, those in the center get the least of the color.

I have this dream often, maybe once or twice a year. It varies. For the most part, this is the overall dream. It's terrifying and spectacular.

www.ingramcontent.com/pod-product-compliance
Lightning Source LLC
Chambersburg PA
CBHW031052020726
47495CB00007B/1845